you are not here

not here

SAMANTHA SCHUTZ

PUSH

GO THERE.

OTHER TITLES
AVAILABLE FROM

Kendra
Coe Booth

Tyrell
Coe Booth

Being
Kevin Brooks

Black Rabbit Summer
Kevin Brooks

Candy
Kevin Brooks

Kissing the Rain
Kevin Brooks

Lucas
Kevin Brooks

Martyn Pig
Kevin Brooks

The Road of the Dead
Kevin Brooks

Ordinary Ghosts
Eireann Corrigan

Splintering
Eireann Corrigan

You Remind Me of You
Eireann Corrigan

Johnny Hazzard
Eddie de Oliveira

Lucky
Eddie de Oliveira

Hail Caesar
Thu-Huong Ha

Born Confused
Tanuja Desai Hidier

Dirty Liar
Brian James

Perfect World
Brian James

Pure Sunshine
Brian James

Thief
Brian James

Tomorrow, Maybe
Brian James

The Dating Diaries
Kristen Kemp

I Will Survive
Kristen Kemp

Beast
Ally Kennen

Heavy Metal and You
Christopher Krovatin

Magic City
Drew Lerman

Cut
Patricia McCormick

Talking in the Dark
Billy Merrell

Losers
Matthue Roth

Never Mind the Goldbergs
Matthue Roth

I Don't Want to Be Crazy
Samantha Schutz

A Little Friendly Advice
Siobhan Vivian

Not That Kind of Girl
Siobhan Vivian

Same Difference
Siobhan Vivian

Learning the Game
Kevin Waltman

Nowhere Fast
Kevin Waltman

Crashing
Chris Wooding

Kerosene
Chris Wooding

Fighting Ruben Wolfe
Markus Zusak

Getting the Girl
Markus Zusak

You Are Here, This Is Now
Edited by David Levithan

Where We Are, What We See
Edited by David Levithan

We Are Quiet, We Are Loud
Edited by David Levithan

This Is PUSH
Edited by David Levithan

Copyright © 2010 by Samantha Schutz

All rights reserved. Published by PUSH, an imprint of Scholastic Inc., publishers since 1920. SCHOLASTIC and associated logos are trademarks and/or registered trademarks of Scholastic Inc.

Library of Congress Cataloging-in-Publication Data Available

ISBN 978-0-545-16911-0

10 9 8 7 6 5 4 3 2 1   10 11 12 13 14

Printed in the U.S.A.   23

First edition, October 2010

The text was set in Rialto DF with Myriad Pro.

Book design by Kristina Iulo

FOR ADRIENNE GLASSER AND WIN ROSENFELD

THANK YOU FOR SHARING YOUR STORIES,

BUT EVEN MORE SO FOR BEING INCREDIBLY

STRONG INDIVIDUALS AND A BRILLIANT COUPLE.

Acknowledgments

I am so grateful to my mother, father, and extended family (the Bennetts, Dosiks, and Greenes) for their support and encouragement; my editor, David Levithan, and the other geniuses at Scholastic for their enthusiasm; my agent, the illustrious Barry Goldblatt; Judy Goldschmidt, for brainstorming with me; and finally, Dr. Stefania Giobbe for her COD expertise.

Special shout-outs to Jessica Schutz, for being a super sister and for helping me work out the kinks; Annica Lydenberg for being my first and favorite reader; and Amy Wilson, Emily Dauber, Emily Haisley, Emily Klein, Lauren Cecil, and Nicole Duncan for their unwavering friendship.

And finally, to my Penguin posse: I never take for granted that I get to spend five days a week with you. You are the kindest, funniest, most creative bunch of people I have ever met.

The "death book" is based, in part, on two fantastic books: I Will Remember You by Laura Dower and Look at the Sky: Death in Cultures Around the World by Shawn Haley.

I walk down my block
and then take a right turn.
Two more blocks
and I'll be with Brian.
For the first time
in a long time,
I know he'll be there
waiting for me.

I sit down on the grass next to him.
He has flowers,
but I know they're not for me.
I wonder who gave them to him,
but I don't ask.

I tell Brian about my day.
I say, "I saw your dad
at the supermarket.
I didn't talk to him —
it's not like he knows who I am,
and even if he did,
I wouldn't know what to say.

I watched him
take things off the shelves,
look them over,
and then put them back.
There was almost nothing

in his cart.
I wonder if he's always been like that,
or just lately."
I say, "I miss you."
I ask if he's missed me too,
then wait for his answer.

If that squirrel runs up that tree,
then his answer is yes.
If it stays on the grass,
his answer is no.

The squirrel doesn't move,
and my breath catches in my throat.
After a moment,
it zips up the tree.
I smile and lie down
next to Brian.
I wish he could hold me
like he used to,
but he doesn't.

The warm sun makes me drowsy
and I fall asleep on my side
next to Brian.
When I wake up, grass is imprinted
on my arm and leg.
I brush myself off,

but Brian doesn't move.
I say, "I'll see you tomorrow."
I reach out to touch him,
and my fingers make contact
with words:

BRIAN DENNIS
DIED AGE SEVENTEEN
BELOVED SON AND FRIEND

Part One

If I do not sleep,
it will not come.
If I do not sleep,
it will not come.
If I do not sleep,
it will not come.

I need this night
to last forever.
I need it to go on
because once I fall asleep,
it will be tomorrow.
It will be the day
of Brian's funeral.
And I can't do that.
I can't see that.
I can't feel that.

My eyes are burning.
They want to seal shut.
They want a break from crying.
My body is sore from tensing,
and it wants release.
It wants the softness of sleep,
but I cannot give it that.
I cannot
let that happen.

I cannot
go from today to tomorrow.

If I do not sleep,
it will not come.
If I do not sleep,
it will not come.
If I do not sleep,
it will not come.

I repeat these nine words
like a mantra.
I try to hold on to them
like worry beads,
like a rosary,
but instead of keeping me focused
they are lulling
me to sleep.

If I do not
sleep it will
not come if I
do not sleep
it will not
come if I do
not sleep it
will not come if
I do not

sleep
it

will

not

come.

Morning light streams in my window.
The air in here is stale.
I need to get out.
Marissa will be here in an hour,
but I can't wait that long.

On my way out of the house,
I pass my mother's bedroom.
Her door is open.
Her bed is perfectly made,
unslept in.

Outside, the late June air
is heavy and hot,
but it's better than in my room.
I'm not sure where I'm going,
but when my flip-flops hit the sidewalk,
I know.

I walk down the street
and take a right turn.
I go two more blocks
and find myself at the cemetery.

It doesn't take long before I hear it —
the sound of dirt and rock
sliding against metal shovels.
There are men digging Brian's grave.

They are digging a hole
in the cool earth, on a hot day
for the boy who has occupied
my thoughts and my heart
for the last three months,
for the boy I lost
my virginity to,
for the boy I think I loved.

I've heard these guys dig before.
I've heard these guys talking,
but today I want to scream
them into silence.
I want to tell them
to have some respect
and not talk
about everyday things,
like how hot it is
or how much more
they have to dig.
This
is not
every day.

This is how I found out:

I was watching a special about the pyramids
when my cell phone vibrated angrily
against my dresser.
I looked at the phone and was surprised
to see Marissa's name.
I flipped open my phone
and cautiously said,
"Hey . . . what's up?"
    "I have to tell you something.
    It's about Brian," Marissa answered.

There was something
about how she said it
that made me think
she was finally going to apologize
and say she had been wrong about him.
But instead she said,
    "Something happened today
    while Brian was playing basketball."
An injury, I figured;
he had a broken leg or something.
But what was with all the drama?
And why was she
calling to tell me?
We hadn't talked in weeks.
    Marissa said, "No one knows
    exactly what happened yet.

But he died, Annaleah.
I am so sorry.
I hate that I am the one
telling you this.
Especially after . . ."

I stopped listening.
My whole body was shuddering.
Uncontrollable.

"What?" I said.
It was the only thing
I could say.
   "My dad was walking the dog
   by the playground
   and saw an ambulance.
   He asked who was hurt
   and they told him it was a teenager
   named Brian Dennis,
   and that he had suddenly died.
   My dad came home and asked me
   if I knew who Brian was."

"What?" I said again.

   "He collapsed on the court.
   The paramedics said
   he died on the spot.

There was nothing
they could do."

Not possible, I thought.
Brian was healthy.
Seventeen.
Just finished his junior year.
How could he be playing
basketball one minute
and then be dead the next?
How could there be no in-between?
No treatment.
No drugs.
No surgery.
No hope.
No nothing.

Not possible.

"Annaleah, are you still there?"
"Uh-huh."

I couldn't even make real words.
I thought, I need to call someone.
I need more information.
But who could I call?
Brian and I didn't have
the same friends.
I could call Joy or Parker,

to tell them what happened,
but they didn't know Brian
other than from my stories.
I could call my mom, but I never
told her Brian and I
were together.
I could call Brian's house
to see if his parents knew more,
but I bet the last thing they'd want
is to talk to a girl
they'd probably never heard of.

    "Annaleah?"
"Yeah. I'm gonna go."
    "Do you want me to come over?"
"No. I'll talk to you later."

I hung up the phone
and looked around my room.
There were pages from magazines
and posters on the wall,
photos of friends,
piles of dirty clothes,
and all of it seemed absurd.
It was absurd
that I had dirty laundry
and that Brian
was dead.

Idiopathic hypertrophic subaortic stenosis.
That's what the *Ledger* said
was the cause of death.
The wall between the chambers
of Brian's heart became thickened
and blocked the flow of blood.
The article said there was no way
to prevent it,
that there would have been
no symptoms,
and that it would have happened
lightning-fast
and without any pain.

They saw IHSS clearly in the autopsy.
There was no doubt about it.
All the rumors that Brian had overdosed
or that there was an outbreak of meningitis
were ruled out.

The thought of Brian on an autopsy table,
cold and alone,
except for a doctor,
makes me want to throw up.
The thought of someone
looking inside of Brian,
holding his heart,
is surreal.

How can a person be
filled with life
and then be empty?
Where does it all go?

I wonder
how many people
are walking around
with something silent
and terribly wrong inside them.
Our bodies are so complex.
So many opportunities
for something to go wrong —
it's amazing that people
aren't dropping dead
on the streets all day long.

I wonder if Brian knew
what was happening.
Was he scared?
Was he in pain?
Did he see his life
flash before his eyes
like in the movies?

I wish I had been there
to hold his hand,
brush the dark hair
away from his cloudy blue eyes,
whisper to him over and over
that he was loved.
But I doubt my face

was the very last one
he'd wanted to see.

Brian and I met

on the first really warm day in March.
The kind of day where you feel
as if your bones are thawing out,
and all you want to do
is be outside.
So I went for a walk
and found a sunny spot by the bay,
where I sat and stared at the water.
I don't know how long I was there,
but it was a while.
When I finally got up,
I heard someone say,
"But I'm not done yet."
I quickly turned around.
Not twenty feet behind me
was a guy about my age.
He was holding a sketchbook
and smiling.
He was cute,
really cute,
with dark brown hair
and blue eyes.

I couldn't believe
that I hadn't heard him
come up behind me.
I couldn't believe

that he had been drawing me
the whole time.
I suddenly became self-conscious.
Had I done anything embarrassing
while I was sitting there,
like pick my nose
or fix a wedgie?

I walked toward him
and looked down at his sketchbook.
There I was,
sitting in profile on the hill.
It mostly looked like me.
The only thing that was different
was that he had put
an imaginary gust of wind in my hair
so that it floated behind me.

"I'm Brian," he said.
  "Annaleah," I replied.
He asked which way I was walking,
and I pointed in the direction of home.
"I'm going that way too," he said.
As we walked, we talked.
We were both juniors.
He went to the nearby high school
and I told him that my school
was a few towns over.

We tried to see
if we knew people in common,
but it didn't work.
Most of my friends
were from school and didn't live nearby.
Most of his friends
were from the neighborhood.

Before we split to go different directions,
he asked for my phone number.
I couldn't believe
how easy this was.
Guys in my school acted
like I didn't exist.
And random guys this cute
never asked for my number.
So I gave it to him.
But he never called.

The next time I saw him
was kind of like the first.
We ran into each other
two weeks later by the bay.
It was only sort of by accident.
After we met,
I started taking walks by the water,
hoping to run into him.

When we talked this time,
it was as easy
as it had been before.

We discovered
that as kids we'd both been obsessed
with Arlene's, the local candy store,
that had since turned into a travel agency.
I told him, "During the summers when I was little,
I hung out at the pool with my friend Marissa.
We were always wandering around barefoot,
and sometimes, without even realizing,
we'd start walking and end up
at Arlene's, more than half a mile away.
That place was magnetic."

    "I know. That candy was like crack.

    They had everything: Sugar Daddies and Babies,

    Charleston Chews, Laffy Taffy, Swedish Fish —"
"And candy lipsticks and cigarettes,
Now 'n' Laters, Nerds, Fireballs, jawbreakers —"

    "The Lemonheads were the best," he said.
"I was more of a Candy Button girl."

    "Gross. You ate paper,"

    he said, giving me a little shove.
I tried to imagine an eight-year-old Brian.
He'd have been scrappy.
Rail thin with scabbed knees.

"Maybe we fought
over the last Laffy Taffy," I said.
    "Maybe . . ."
This time when we parted,
he promised to call
and he did.

Our first date
wasn't much of a date.
Not that Brian ever actually
used the word "date."
When he finally called,
he asked me to "hang out."

That afternoon, our conversation
was like an epic road trip —
but with no map to guide us
and all the time in the world
to get where we were going.
We meandered, lost our way,
doubled back.

It was nice not having
any friends in common.
I felt like I could be me
without all the crap
that came with me.
I could just show Brian
the parts of me that I wanted.
So I didn't mention my dad,
or that my longest relationship
had been for three weeks
in camp to a boy who kissed
like he was searching my mouth
for something he'd lost,

or that even though senior year was looming,
I had only skimmed the college catalogs
my mom had been stacking on my desk.

Instead I said,
"I'm reading *The Bell Jar* by Sylvia Plath.
But it's going really slowly."
        "Why?" he asked. "Too boring?"
"No. The opposite.
It's so amazing that I have to stop
every few pages to read passages twice."
The topic of crazy people reminded Brian
of the hysterical laughing fits
he has while watching *Family Guy*.
        "I can watch that show for hours
        without even taking a bathroom break."
"I'm that way about documentaries —
especially ones about ancient Egypt or the ocean."
That led us to talking about vacations.
"A few years ago, my mom and I
went to Mexico, and while I was snorkeling,
I got the worst sunburn of my life.
A few days later, my back started peeling.
I looked like a molting reptile or something."
        "That's freaking disgusting.
        But get this: I was at a concert last month
        and this huge, tattooed guy

had an iguana on his shoulder.
I almost barfed up my beer."
"Do you go to concerts a lot?"
The only concert I had ever been to
was the American Idol tour a few years ago.
And that was with Marissa and both our moms.
Not something I wanted to brag about.
"Yeah. I try to.
Nothing's better than leaning against a speaker
and feeling the bass vibrate
through my body."
Which eventually led him to
"This one night, my friend Peter and I were
at a show in the city and missed the last train home.
So we wandered around the Lower East Side,
bought bread still hot from a bakery oven,
and watched the sun rise up over the East River.
I think it was one of the best nights of my life."
That afternoon felt like
one of the best days
of my life.

Brian and I went on like that for weeks.
We'd go for walks or hang out
at whoever's house had no parents.
We'd listen to music,
rarely do homework,

and mostly hook up.
He never drew me again
after that first day at the bay,
and I always wished
he had.

At home, I can't stop
looking in the mirror
at the circles under my green eyes,
the splotchy skin, matted curly hair.
Today is definitely not
a day for mascara.
It's not even a day
that I should be thinking
about my face
or what I am going to wear.

I look in the mirror again
and think, Brian
will never cry again
or have red eyes.
He will never laugh
or kiss
me again.

We had our first kiss
on the sidewalk
in front of my house.

As Brian leaned in,
things disappeared
one by one.
The trees.
The houses.
The cars.
The sidewalk.
Gone.

There was just
my breath
and his.
His lips
on mine.

I've never been to a funeral,
unless you count all the times
I buried pet hamsters
or baby birds that had fallen
from their nests.
But I've been visiting this cemetery
since I was little.
I don't know how old it is,
but the oldest date legible
on the gravestones is 1831.
Some stones are so old
that I can't read the writing —
time has rubbed them clean.
I like running my hands over those,
and wondering
what they once said.

But it's different
when I see gravestones for babies
that had barely lived.
When I see those,
I can't stop thinking
about how tiny and light
the caskets must have been
or how their mothers must have sounded
as they watched those caskets
disappear beneath the earth.

It's getting late.
I need to take a shower
and get dressed.
The shower is a good place to hide.
You can't hear the phone ring in there
or see that you have seven new texts
and four new voicemails.
Your friends cannot ask how you are.
They cannot look at you
with their pity faces.
They cannot hear you cry.
No one can see your tears,
not even you.

Brian is the only person
that I've ever taken a shower with.
It hadn't occurred to me
how different it would be
from being naked while lying down.
In the shower, the lights are on,
your makeup is running off,
your hair is flat against your head.
There is nowhere
and nothing
to hide.

After a few minutes,
I got over it
and we took turns under the showerhead,
splashed water at each other,
and washed each other's backs.
It reminded me of being a kid at the pool —
the playfulness, the games,
the water in my eyes
making everything blurry.

When Brian looked at me
and said, "Turn around,"
I did, but I was wrong
about what he wanted to do.
I could feel his mostly hairless chest,
warm against the back of my shoulders,

as I waited
for something to happen.

I was surprised to hear the sound
of shampoo squirting out of the bottle
and to feel a cold blob of it
landing on my head.
I turned around and gave Brian a squinty look.

"What do you think you're doing?"
I asked playfully.
    "Turn around," he said with a smile.

How could something I do
almost every day without thinking
be so amazing
when someone else did it for me?
"That feels nice," I said
as he massaged my scalp
and lathered the shampoo
through the tangle of dark hair
that fell to the middle of my back.

    "Lean your head into me," he said
as he guided my head under the water
and rinsed off the shampoo,
being careful
not to get soap in my eyes.

Next he put in the conditioner
and combed it through with his fingers.
He rinsed my hair again, then wrung it out.
He did this
without saying
a single word.
But I didn't need any.
I understood his silence.

After my shower,
I start to get dressed for the funeral.
I know I'm supposed to wear black,
but that seems too ordinary.
Everyone will be wearing black
and I
am not
everyone.

I start with underwear.
I open my drawer and see
the light blue ones with bumblebees.
I smile.
Brian liked those.
That was one of our jokes.
The first time we really hooked up,
he was wearing boxers
with lobsters on them.
The second time,
he had on ones with polar bears.
I couldn't stop laughing
because I thought he only wore
boxers with animals on them.
He swore it was a coincidence
and that those were his only two,
but I always made fun of him for it.

I look in my closet
and settle on wearing
a dark purple skirt, a black shirt,
and the bumblebee underwear.

Marissa is waiting for me

in front of my house
so we can walk
to the funeral together.
She's way more freckled from the sun
than the last time I saw her.
She is wearing a black skirt,
black shirt, and sporty silver sandals.
Her thick, straight, blond hair
is pulled into a simple ponytail.
I bet she didn't have to think
about what to wear.
She's a pro.
Both her grandmothers died last year.

I push open the screen door
and walk outside.
Marissa has been meeting me
at my front door
since we were little.
But never
for something like this.
"Annaleah . . .
are you ready?" she asks.
I hang my head down,
shake it.
I am not
ready.

Marissa and I

met at the local pool
when we were five.
It was the same summer
that my mom and I moved here.
The story goes:
One of us had a box of Nerds.
The other one asked for some.
Nerds were shared.
Best friends status was established.
We can never agree
which one of us had the candy.
She insists it was me,
but that's not how I remember it.

And since then,
we've had sleepovers,
told secrets,
and talked on the phone
late into the night.
We were together when we
smoked our first cigarette,
stole lipsticks from the drugstore,
watched horror movies that made us scream,
once laughed so hard
that we actually pissed ourselves,
and blew out birthday candles
for the last eleven years in a row.

But walking to the cemetery
for Brian's funeral
is not
something I thought
we would ever do.

Marissa slips her arm in mine

and we begin.
Each time I take a step,
it feels like I am not
making any progress —
like someone is pulling the church
farther and farther away from me.
But it doesn't matter
how I feel.
Marissa moves me forward.
She is in charge of my body.
And even though this is the first time
I have seen or talked to her in weeks,
I could not imagine doing this
with anyone but her.

As we enter the church,
I walk past a bunch of guys
that I've seen Brian hang around with,
but never officially met.
I look at them and wonder,
Did Brian ever talk about me?
Do you even know who I am?
One of the guys looks up as I walk by.
He holds my gaze for a moment,
but then looks down again.
His eyes tell me nothing.

Marissa only met Brian twice,
both times briefly,
and I wonder if his funeral
counts as the third time.

Since Brian and I started
hanging out a few months ago,
Marissa's listened to me complain
about how Brian would disappear
for days and not call.
How he'd forget we made plans.
How sometimes I felt
like I was just a girl
he wanted to make out with,
not make a future with.

But there were good things
about Brian too.
Marissa never seemed
to want to hear about them.
She insisted
that I was wasting my time with him.
So when Marissa refused
to listen to any more of my stories,
I talked to Joy or Parker.
Like when I told them about
the time Brian's parents went on vacation,

and I lied and told my mom
that I was sleeping at Joy's.

That night Brian and I
got into his bed and watched
A Clockwork Orange, his favorite movie.
The house was silent except for the TV
and our occasional voices.
I pretended it was our house.
That we were married.
That he loved me.
And I wondered,
Is this how it might feel
one day for real?
Perfect and normal.
I wished it would always be like this —
ordinary.

In the morning,
we sat at his dining room table
and ate Cinnamon Toast Crunch.
He brought out the bowls and spoons,
and I brought out the milk.

Up until then,
I'd only seen Brian eat pizza and chips —
things that didn't require utensils.

So I was surprised
to see how he held his spoon.
Instead of just curling his pointer finger
around the spoon's stem,
he used his middle finger too.
It was really cute.
I don't know why, but it was.
Maybe because it made him seem
like a little kid
or maybe because now I knew
one of his subtle quirks.
And that made him closer to me.

All eyes are on Brian.
His casket is up by the altar.
It's the first thing I see
when we walk in
and it's impossible
not to stare right at it —
especially because it's open.
Marissa asks,
"Do you want to say good-bye?"
Her question is ridiculous.
I said good-bye to Brian
after we hung out
a few days ago.
He was fine.
There was no reason to think
I would never see him again.

I want to see Brian
and I don't.
I haven't seen him in days
and I miss him —
miss his face.
But I'm scared.
Scared of what he'll look like.
Scared because this means it's over.
That he is gone.
That he is not
coming back.
This is a different kind
of good-bye.

Marissa's arm is linked with mine.
It has not shifted
since we met at my house.
I feel her grip tighten a little
as we walk down the aisle.
We are like a father and bride
on her wedding day.
We move slowly.
Both anticipating,
and maybe also fearing,
what is at the end
of this slow, careful march.
But my father and I
will never
take this walk.
And all the fantasies
I've had of Brian
meeting me at the altar
never looked like this.

As we get closer to him,
I feel my face and body start to burn.
It's a cold burn.
My body is prickling.
It feels like there are spines
poking through my skin.
I used to get a similar feeling
whenever I'd get near Brian.

But this is different.
It used to be pleasant, tingly.
This is painful, sharp.

I look down into the casket.
My stomach contracts.
Is that really Brian?
He doesn't look right.
It's like a wax version of him.
His coloring is off.
He's in a suit.
There is a cross around his neck.
I am inches from him,
but there is no smell.
No clean laundry.
No deodorant.
No hair gel.
Nothing.
There is
nothing.

I do not feel
Marissa's arm.
I do not feel
the floor.
I do not feel
my body.

I want to burrow into his neck
and feel the warmth,
but this Brian looks cold.
This Brian
isn't the one I know.

Throughout the service
I can't decide if I feel
like my body is hollow,
light like a balloon,
or if I feel like my bones
are filled with cement.

I can't decide if I am going
to drift up off the pew, into the air,
and bump into the ceiling,
or if my weight will send me crashing
through the pew, then floor, then earth
and I won't stop falling
until I am deep underground
like Brian is about to be.

I put my head on Marissa's shoulder
and look over at the casket again.
The box is smaller
than I thought it would be.
I want to lie down next to it
to measure.

I look at the podium
and see people speaking.
I see kids my age,
some adults, and a woman
I assume is Brian's mother.
I see their mouths move,
but there is no sound.
It is a silent movie.

The one time
that I sort of met Brian's dad
didn't go how I'd hoped it would.

"Shit," Brian said
as he looked out his bedroom window.
This was several weeks ago.
"He wasn't supposed to be home
for another hour.
You need to go."
   "Now?"
"Yes."
   "Right now?"
"Yes."
He handed me my bag.

I had never met either of Brian's parents.
He usually ushered me out
before they got home.
I didn't understand why.
Brian was always talking about
staying out all night.
Surely if his parents could handle that,
they wouldn't mind
him having a girl in his room.
But maybe they weren't the problem.
Maybe he was ashamed of me.

I took my bag from Brian,
put on my sneakers,
and followed him down the stairs.
I thought
maybe this made us even.
Brian had never met my mom either.

As we walked past the living room
and to the front door,
I caught a glimpse
of Brian's dad on the couch.
His necktie was loosened,
he had a beer in one hand,
and the TV remote in the other.
He didn't even look up
as we walked by.

There was a moment
of awkward silence
as I stood on the stoop with Brian.
I filled it with
"So, that's the man
who made you?"
    "He
    didn't
    make
    me."

I bit my lip.
I had never heard Brian
speak in that tone before
He said good-bye,
then shut the door.

Maybe it wasn't me
he was ashamed of.

People are standing.
Marissa is lightly pulling me
up and toward the door.
People are filing out,
hugging, touching.
I hardly recognize anyone.
I wish there were more people
who knew me here.
That way they could hold me too,
stroke my hair
and tell me they know
how much it hurts.
But there isn't anyone
besides Marissa.

When Marissa and I walk out of the church,
the summer sun is blinding.
The insides of the church
were white and cool.
Now everything is painfully bright.
The blue sky, green grass,
and yellow sun are like jewels.
But then I see
all those flat gray stones.

We all parade to the spot
that's been dug for Brian.
The ground is uneven
and it's hard to stand.
But maybe that's just me.

We are each given a single white rose
and then the priest starts up again.
But I'm not listening.
I'm staring at the rose, thinking,
How long before
this flower starts to wilt?
How long before Brian starts to . . .
I look away.
I shouldn't think
these things.

Brian's mom is wailing.
She can barely support
her own weight.
It's like she has no bones.
Brian's dad is at her side,
trying to support her.
That's when I notice
that he and Brian
have the same cloudy blue eyes.

There are loads of kids here.
Most are huddled together,
holding hands,
sniffling, crying.
I always wanted
to hang out with Brian's friends,
to have him introduce me
as his girlfriend.
But neither of those things ever happened.
And now there's no one
to introduce me.
No one
to confirm the way that I knew Brian.
It's like I,
we,
didn't exist.

When the priest is done
reciting prayers, he says,
"And now, Brian's best friend, Peter,
would like to say a few additional words."
Peter steps forward.
He is holding a piece of paper.
I look to see if his hand shakes.
It doesn't.

"This is a poem by Henry Scott Holland.
'Death is nothing at all.
I have only slipped away into the next room.
I am I and you are you.
Whatever we were to each other,
That we are still.
Call me by my old familiar name.
Speak to me in the easy way you always used.
Put no difference into your tone.
Wear no forced air of solemnity or sorrow.
Laugh as we always laughed
at the little jokes we enjoyed together.
Play, smile, think of me. Pray for me.
Let my name be ever the household word
that it always was.
Let it be spoken without effort.
Without the ghost of a shadow on it.
Life means all that it ever meant.
It is the same as it ever was.

There is absolute unbroken continuity.
What is death but a negligible accident?
Why should I be out of mind
because I am out of sight?
I am but waiting for you for an interval
Somewhere very near
Just around the corner.
All is well.'"

That is it.
That is where he stops.

After everyone tosses their rose
into Brian's grave
we begin to walk away.
Marissa gives my arm a little squeeze
and asks, "Do you want to go
to the after-thing?
It's at Brian's house."

There are ghosts in this house.
Brian is one.
I am another.
But Brian is all over this house.
There are photos.
There are memories of him
that are collectively shared
by friends and family.

I am a different kind of ghost.
There are no traces of me here
except for my fingerprints.
Brian was the only other person
who shared my memories here.
And now that he's gone,
I am their sole keeper.

Marissa gets up to go to the bathroom

and an older woman sits down next to me.
She's got the same cloudy blue eyes
as Brian and his dad.
She turns to me and extends her hand.
"I'm Freda, Brian's grandmother."
    "Annaleah," I say as I take her hand.
Her skin is transparent
like tracing paper, but soft and warm.
Mountainous veins ridge her hand.
"You all are too young for this,"
she says, then sips her water.
"When I lost Joey, my husband,
there was warning.
He was sick. Old.
But Brian.
So sudden. So sudden."
She sips again.
"Did you and Brian go to school together?"
    "No. I — We —"
I can't even begin to explain,
but her eyes seem to understand.
Could Brian have told her about me?
She slides her hand over mine.
Strokes it.
It feels so different
from Marissa's.

Marissa's hand is firm.
This hand is light.
It slides over mine like silk.

Brian's dad is sitting on the deck.
All I can see is his back.
He's got a cigarette in one hand,
a beer in the other,
and a lot of empties at his feet.

Brian's dad didn't speak at the funeral,
and I haven't seen or heard him talking
to anyone this afternoon.
And since I always called Brian on his cell,
I've never even heard his dad's voice.
Maybe he doesn't have one.

I want to get away from all these strangers.
I want to sit on Brian's bed and pretend
that it's four o'clock after school.

Brian's windows are open
and the late spring breeze
makes the curtains expand
and contract.
His mom is working late
and his dad won't be home
for a few hours.
We are both sitting on his bed,
but on opposite ends.
We are listening to music.
Brian is drawing in his sketchbook.
I am writing in my English journal,
but I don't let him look
since it's about him.
He comes closer to my end of the bed,
tries to see what I'm writing.
I swat him away,
close the covers,
and slip the book back in my bag.
He smiles and leans in toward me.
A chunk of hair falls over his left eye.
His lips touch mine.
His hands are on my face,

then my neck,
my shoulders,
my chest.
Buttons are undone.
I am undone.

I had been waiting
for the right time
for a long time.
I had been waiting
for romance,
for candles,
for rose petals.
But when the time came,
I hadn't even shaved my legs,
and I wasn't wearing fancy underwear.
It just happened.
After weeks of saying no,
I said yes.

I thought that afterward
I would cry
or do something dramatic.
I thought
I would feel different,
but I didn't.
It was everything around me
that felt different.
As I walked home
from Brian's that afternoon,
I suddenly felt connected
to the birds, to the trees,
to the people around me.
I felt a part of everything.

Not including the day Brian died,

Marissa and I have only spoken twice
in the last few weeks.
The first conversation,
the one that deepened
the already growing rift,
went like this:

"You did what?" she asked.
    "We did it," I said.
"Is he even your boyfriend?"
    "Not exactly."
"Did he say 'I love you?'"
    "No."
"Did you?"
    "No."
"How do you feel?"
    "Okay."
"Did it hurt?"
    "Not really."
"Well, at least that's something."
    "Why are you being like this?"
"Like what?"
    "Like a bitch.

    Can't you just be happy for me?"
"All you do is complain
about Brian.
And now you have sex with him?

Good plan, Annaleah.
I don't want to hear about it
when you start freaking out.
Because if you do,
it'll be your own fault."
    "I can't believe you.
    You don't even know him.
    You're probably just jealous
    that I had sex and you didn't."
"Hardly, Annaleah.
Hardly."
    "Thanks for the support, Maris."

It bothers me that I can't remember
all the details
of the last time Brian and I had sex.
I didn't know
it would be the last time.
If I had,
I would have traced Brian's face,
run my fingers over his eyelids,
nose, and mouth.
I would have connected
his freckles and beauty marks,
memorized them
like a star chart.
I would have ruffled his soft, dark hair,
run my hands over his chest and arms.
I would have held him
tightly —
measured the space
he took up in my arms.
I would have
nestled into his neck,
smelled him,
taken all of him in —
enough to make it last
my whole life.

I can't
stop thinking
that Brian and I
never
danced.
I don't know why
it sticks out so much,
but it does.

The last time Marissa and I talked
before the day Brian died,
went about as well as when
I told her Brian and I
slept together.

She called and said,
"Hey. How are you?"
　　"Okay," I answered.
"And Brian?"
That was new.
She never asked about him.
　　"Good. I saw him a few days ago."
"I saw him today."
She said those four words so quickly
they practically blurred.
　　"Oh. Cool.
　　Did you say hi?"
"No. He was with some girl in the park.
She was blond and really pretty."
　　"Oh.
　　Okay."
"They looked cozy."
Was she trying to start a fight?
Because this was a great way to do that.
　　"It could have just been a friend, Maris."
"Or not.
Have you talked about being exclusive yet?"

"Maris, what are you doing?
We haven't spoken in a while
and *this* is what you call me to say?"
"I'm trying to get you to see
that he's not good for you."
"Well, this conversation
doesn't feel like it's
any good for me."
"I thought you should know."
"Well, now I know.
Thanks."
And I hung up.

I tried not to think about what Marissa said,
but that night I called Brian
and asked what he had done that day.
His answer was,
"I slept late and then hung out with Peter."
Maybe he didn't mention the girl
because he thought I would get the wrong idea.
Or maybe it was because Marissa was right
and something was going on.
It made me sick to think about,
so I just stopped thinking.

Marissa comes back from the bathroom

and wants to know
my plans for the rest of the afternoon.
Do I want to hang out and talk,
watch a movie, go for a walk?
All I want
is to go upstairs to Brian's room.
I want to open his window
and sit on his bed,
but I can't.
It doesn't feel right
with all these people here.
Without Brian here.

I want
to say something
to Brian's friends and family,
but I don't.
What would I say?
"Hello, I'm the girl
who was in love with Brian.
Oh? You haven't heard of me?
That's because we weren't really dating."

Instead, I leave with Marissa.

On the way upstairs to my bedroom,
I pause to look at the photos on the wall.
There's one of my mom's parents
on their wedding day.
Both of them died before I was born.
My mom says I look like my grandma,
but I don't see it.
There's a photo of my mom
the day she graduated nursing school.
There's one of me as a baby,
sitting on a man's lap.
My whole hand is curled
around one of his fingers.
You can't see his face —
just his hand and his crotch.
This is my father,
Robert Rollins,
and it is the only picture of him
on display in our house.

He left when I was only a year old.
My mom almost never talks about him.
She says that the last thing
they ever agreed on was my name.
She wanted Anna.
He wanted Leah.

Every day at Sacred Heart Hospital,

my mother helps people heal.

She gives them comfort.

She listens to them.

She sees

them.

But I do not think

she sees

me.

This time,

when I walk past my mom's room
she is in bed,
back from the night shift.
She rolls over when she hears me pass
and groggily says,
"Annaleah, did you go
to that boy's funeral?"

    I nod and say, "With Marissa."
As I walk over to her bed she says,
"Glad to see you and Marissa
are talking again.
It's been a while.
I hope that whatever came between you
isn't a problem anymore."

She takes in and lets out
a deep breath before continuing,
"Do you know how rare it is
for a healthy seventeen-year-old boy
to die from IHSS?"
I do.
I looked it up online.
"Well, that was nice of you to go.
This is such a small community.
I'm sure his parents were glad
that so many people turned out."

She shifts over,
then pulls back the covers for me.
"Wanna get in?" she asks.
I slip in next to her.
We've never done this.
I wonder if she knows
that I was lying when I said
that I only knew Brian in passing.
I wonder if she's waiting for me
to tell her everything,
but I don't.
I can't.

My mom falls back into sleep
easily, but I don't.
Instead, I think of my father.
He lives in Los Angeles.
He is remarried
to a woman named Lauren.
They have twin seven-year-old girls,
Lisa and Sage.

My father is an engineer.
He likes to golf.
He is training for a marathon.
He also likes to cook,
but is terrible at it.

Lauren teases him,
says his best meal is buttered toast.

I tell myself these things
when I miss my dad.
They are a lullaby
that calms me to sleep.

I wake up a little while later

and find my mom, freshly showered,
in my room, stripping my bed.
"What are you doing?" I ask.
    "Laundry."
"Stop."
She doesn't seem to hear me
because she's still tugging
the sheet off the bed.
"Stop." I say it louder.
She stares at me, confused,
as she shakes a pillow out of its case.
"Stop!" I scream.
"You're never here.
You never do anything mom-like.
Why are you starting now?"
She drops the pillow to the floor
and kicks her way out of the room,
wading through the pile of linens
like high tide.
    "Fine, Annaleah.
    Do it yourself."

I fall into the pile
and tears roll down my cheeks.
I raise a handful of cotton to my nose.
Can I still catch a bit of Brian?
Can I still smell him

from the last time he was in my bed?
All I can smell is me
and maybe a little bit
of my mom's shampoo in the air.

I go to my dresser
and pull out a T-shirt
that Brian left here weeks ago,
a drawing he gave me,
a postcard from the Metropolitan Museum of Art,
and the article about Brian from the paper.
It isn't much.
But it's all I have.

I look down at the postcard
that I got at the Met with Brian.
It's a painting of a ghost-like man
wearing purple and white robes,
sitting on a throne.
His mouth is open.
Teeth exposed, screaming.
He looks like he's behind bars.
The artist is Francis Bacon.

One Sunday in May,
Brian asked me to go with him
to the Bacon exhibit at the Met.

We go to the railroad station,
buy tickets, and sit on a bench,
drinking too-sweet coffee
as we wait for the train.

While sitting there, I think,
This is it.
Things are changing.
Going to the city to see art
is what couples do.

On the train, Brian uses his phone
to show me some of Bacon's paintings.

I put my head on his shoulder
and watch as he gently drags
his finger across the screen
over and over again.
Bacon's stuff is really creepy,
all twisted bodies and swollen faces.
But I don't say anything.
Brian seems really into it.

When we get off the railroad,
we transfer to the E, then the 6 train.
I don't know how to get to the Met,
but Brian does —
without even looking at a map.
He says it's because he goes
to galleries and museums all the time.
I didn't know that.

When we get off the subway
we cross Lexington, Park,
Madison, and Fifth.
The apartments get more and more amazing
the closer we get to the museum.
Some people have their curtains open,
and you can see right in.
Giant mirrors, paintings,
floor-to-ceiling bookshelves, colorful walls.
I wonder if maybe one day,

I'll live like that.
That maybe we'll
live like that.
I know it's not realistic,
but it's never fun
to be realistic.

As we walk around the exhibit,
Brian talks, and I listen.
He says, "I like Bacon's paintings
because they remind me
of my nightmares."
I wonder, What's going on
that this
is what you dream about?
I want to ask him,
but I can't get out the words.
I think it would be pushing my luck
on what is already a monumental day.

When we finish the exhibit,
I tell Brian that I want
to check out the Egyptian wing.
There's this one tomb
that I remember seeing with my mom
when I was a kid.
At the time, I was sure
that a mummy would jump out

and try to kill me.
I want to see how it looks now,
nearly ten years later.

The tomb is laughably small.
When Brian and I walk inside,
he takes my hand
and jokingly says,
"I'll protect you."
And even though
he is just messing around,
I take a moment to breathe in his words.
Joking or not,
he never says things like that to me.

As we walk down the short corridor
and make the only turn,
Brian shouts, "Boo!"
I let out a scream —
one that is much louder
than I would have liked.
"I couldn't resist,"
he says, laughing.
    "You're a jerk," I say,
    shoving him in the chest.
He quickly covers my hand with his,
pressing my palm flat against his chest.

"I'm sorry," he says.
Then he kisses me,
his warm sweet breath a contrast
to the stale coolness
of the tomb.

At home,
I check my voicemail.

"Lee. It's Parker.
Thinking about you.
Call me."

"Hey, babe. It's Joy.
I guess you're not picking up.
We should hang out
and do something.
Or do nothing.
Whatever you want.
Just call me.
Love you."

I hit the DELETE button.
I do not
call either of them back.

The last time I talked to Joy

was the weekend before Brian died.
She asked me if I wanted to go
to the movies with her and Parker.

"What are you seeing?"
    "A Miyazaki film."
"I don't know.
Anime's not my thing.
Plus, Brian and I
might be doing something."
    "Might?"
"Yeah. We talked earlier
and he said maybe
we'd do something later.
That he'd call me."
    "Lee."
"What?"
    "Come with us.
    Or call Brian and invite him,
    but don't sit home and wait
    for his call.
    He's not worth
    ruining your night over."
"I'm not.
I won't."
But I was
and probably would be.

"All right, it's your call.
Movie's not until nine,
so call me if you change your mind.
We'll even pick you up.
And Parker says he'll pay for you."
"Okay. Thanks.
Talk to you later."

6:00
Nothing.

7:00
Nothing.

8:00
Nothing.

8:15
I could've probably
still asked Parker and Joy to pick me up.

8:30
I could've still
called a cab and gotten to the movie in time.

9:00
I decided I didn't want to see that anime shit anyway.

I've been trying to sleep for hours.
I've seen the minute hand
go around and around many times.
I flip over on my stomach,
bury my face in the pillow
and cry.
I think about screaming,
but I bet the sound
only gets muffled in the movies,
not in real life.
I settle for kicking my legs up and down,
letting them bang against my mattress
like a fish trying to swim out of water —
but I'm getting nowhere.
I flip over to my back,
then get out of bed.

I turn on the bathroom light
and it burns my eyes.
I squint and look in the mirror.
Pimples dot my forehead.
I go for the whiteheads first.
I pop and squeeze until there is blood.
Then I move on to my cheeks and chin.

I don't know how long
I've been standing there,

but my legs are stiff and hurt.
My face is blotchy.
It's obvious
that I've made my skin worse,
but I feel like I was productive.
Like I just did
something.

I go back to my room
and look at the clock.
It's been forty-five minutes.
Forty-five minutes of not thinking
about Brian.
Not wondering what life
will be like without him,
even though I never really knew
what life was like
with him.

I get back into bed.
The only sound I can hear
are the crickets.
But then there's a sound
at my window.
I know it's probably just a branch,
but still I get up to look.
There is nothing besides

the streetlamp casting a glow
in the spot where Brian stood
a few weeks ago.

On that night, I had heard
the sound of pebbles
smacking against glass.
I got out of bed
and looked out my window.
There, underneath the streetlamp,
was Brian.
I could see him grinning,
even from two stories up.
I pushed open my window
and whispered as loudly as I could,
"Are you crazy?"
    "Yes. Come down."
And I did.

As I walked across the wet grass
and into the street,
Brian looked me over
in my boxers and thin tank top.
    "You're not wearing a bra."
"It's hot. And I was sleeping."
He pulled me toward him,
his hands firm on my lower back.

His kiss was warm and wet
and tasted like beer.
I pulled back.

"Are you drunk?"
    "No."
But then I saw a forty-ounce beer at his feet.
"I'm going back to bed."
    "But I wanted to see you . . .
    to tell you . . ."
But he stopped.
He always stopped.
I waited for a moment,
but nothing else came.

"I'm going back to bed."
As I walked away,
Brian didn't try to stop me.
I quietly closed the front door
and went up the stairs.
I brushed off my feet
before getting back into bed
and wondered
how I was going to fall asleep now.
My body was tense
with energy, frustration.
I curled my toes,
stretched out my legs,

balled my hands into tight fists,
lengthened my arms,
raised my shoulders to my ears,
squeezed my eyes shut,
then released
with one long exhale.

Just as I was wondering
if Brian was still out there,
I heard a bottle shatter
against the pavement.
I guess that was my answer.

For the next five days
Brian didn't call
to apologize.
He didn't send me
an email,
an IM,
or a text.
He didn't do anything.
He never did
anything.

It doesn't make sense

that today is a typical summer morning.
The sky is cloudless.
Kids are riding their bikes.
People are gardening.
But today is not an ordinary day.
It is the day after Brian's funeral.

The sky should be black.
Lightning should knife
through the air.
There should be blasts of thunder.
Rain should fall in bullets
and shatter windshields.

"Hey. It's Marissa.
I'm wondering
how you're feeling
and what you're up to today.
I know things have been weird between us,
but I'm here for you.
Talk to you soon."

I hit the DELETE button
and do not call her back.

I leave the house
to go for a walk around the bay.
I used to do this a lot.
Sometimes it was just to get air,
but mostly it was to find Brian.
Usually, this tactic didn't work
and I would come home disappointed,
but there were a few times
that I did find him.
Those times, I always thought,
Why didn't you call me?
I live a few blocks away.
I could have hung out with you.
Why would you rather be alone
than be with me?

Now as I walk through the neighborhood,
I see Brian on the hill by the bay,
hunched over a notebook, drawing.
I see him on the basketball court —
the very place he died —
taking shots.
It was only about a month ago
that I found Brian right here.

> He spots me,
> lifts up his shirt
> and wipes the sweat from his face,

revealing his smooth stomach
and the trail of dark hair
that disappears into his shorts.
I try not to stare.

"What's going on?" he asks.
    "Nothing. Just needed
    to get out of the house."
But that's not really true.
"Yeah. My house
was feeling kinda tight too.
My dad's home."
I know better than to say anything.
I wait, giving Brian room to continue.

"Wanna play?" he asks.
    "I'm not any good.
    And besides,
    I'm wearing flip-flops."
"It's okay.
Just take them off."

I walk over to the edge of the court
and put my flip-flops on the grass.
I carefully walk back across the warm concrete,
being sure to look for broken glass.

"Can you dribble?" he asks
as he passes me the ball.

Thank God I catch it.
I would have felt like such an ass.
I dribble a few times.
"Okay, not bad," he says.
"Can you shoot?"
I take a shot.
It's not great,
but at least it comes close
and hits the backboard.

Brian runs after the ball
and passes it back to me.
"Try again. But this time
follow through with your wrist."
    "Okay, coach."
When I try again,
I make the shot.
"Nice," he says
as he catches the ball.

I take a few more shots.
Each time, Brian gives me tips
and encouragement.
I make enough of the shots
to be pretty pleased with myself.

"I think it's time
for some one-on-one."

"Seriously?"
Brian plays basketball
nearly every day.
　"I don't know.
　That couldn't be much fun for you."
"It's okay.
I'll take my chances."

Brian passes me the ball
and I start dribbling,
making my way toward the basket.
Brian comes at me
and reaches for the ball.
It's obvious he isn't trying his hardest.
When I turn my back to him,
he leans over me —
almost like we're spooning
while shuffling back and forth.
My back is pressed against him.
I can feel how warm he is.
I can feel the sweat on his arms.
But Brian seems to get bored
with not trying
because he finally reaches around
and steals the ball.

In one smooth move,
he pivots, shoots the ball,

and makes the basket.
"Show-off,"
I say with a smile.

When the memory fades,
so does my smile.
I am alone
on this court.

The second night after Brian's funeral
is like the first.
On my stomach.
On my side.
On my back.
Curled up in a ball.
Diagonally.
My feet at the head of the bed.
Blanket on.
Blanket off.
TV on.
TV off.
Music on.
Music off.

I cannot sleep.
I cannot stop
this waking nightmare.
I want to dream.
I want to dream of Brian.

I put my pillow over my face,
take a deep breath,
and try to smell Brian.
I imagine him in my room,
talking,
walking,
smiling,

laughing,
lying next to me,
kissing me,
touching me.

I watch as the shadows
move quietly across my walls,
just like he used to move
across my room.
I look at them, searching
for his shape.
Will he come to me?
Will I hear his voice
one more time?
I squeeze my eyes shut.
I imagine his face, his body.
I am trying to will him
into appearing,
but he doesn't.

All those talk-show psychics
make it seem like this should be easier.
People all over the place
are connecting with the dead.
Why can't I?
Maybe Brian
doesn't want to visit me.
Maybe I

am not important enough.
Or maybe, right now,
Brian is hovering over
his parents or close friends,
giving them comfort.
Maybe he's so busy with them
that he's forgotten about me.
Or maybe it's just not my turn
yet.

Part Two

I had a dream last night

that Marissa and I were in a taxi
driving on an overpass.
The driver took a turn way too fast
and lost control of the car.
We jumped the guardrail
and soared through the air,
hundreds of feet above the ground.
I knew we were going to die.
I thought about calling my mom
to tell her I loved her,
but there was no time.
Then the taxi became a convertible,
and Marissa fell out of the car.
I caught her sleeve for a second,
but I couldn't hold her.
I watched her fall
and fall, then hit
the street below.
It was all happening in slow motion.
I knew
I was about to die,
and I couldn't do anything
but watch the pavement
get closer
and closer.

It takes a lot of harassing texts,
but Parker and Joy convince me
to leave the house
and watch the Fourth of July fireworks
down by the bay.

Parker and Joy
are like an old married couple.
They finish each other's sentences
and bicker all the time.
Except one big difference
is that Parker is gay,
and Joy falls in love
with every guy she meets.

When we all meet up,
Joy looks adorable.
She's wearing a vintage dress
and her red hair is twisted into two little buns.
Parker's wearing longish jean shorts
and, as usual, he's got on a funny T-shirt.
This one says BLAH, BLAH, BLAH.
I look down at my own outfit.
There's nothing cute
about my dirty jeans and plain white tank.
It's pretty much a miracle
that I'm out of my house
and not in my pj's.

We pick a spot on the seawall
that can't be seen from the road,
and dangle our legs over the edge,
waiting for the show to start.

Joy tells us about the new guy
she's been talking to.
Parker tells us about the trip
he's going to take with his family
to the Grand Canyon.
Their lives are moving forward.
Mine is stagnant.

The first fireworks blast knocks
these thoughts from my head.
For a moment, the black sky is lit up
with a shower of sparks
and we are all temporarily cast in red.
All I can think of is blood.
Brian's heart bursting.
Tears well up in my eyes
and I'm glad
that Parker and Joy
are looking at the fireworks
and not at me.

When the tears pool over,
I wipe them away,
then take a sip of warm beer.

If Brian were alive,
what would he be doing tonight?
Would he be here
with his arm around my shoulder?
As we watched the fireworks,
would he kiss my neck
and whisper to me
that I smelled good?
Or would he be somewhere else,
watching with his friends,
and getting drunk or stoned?
The second scenario sounds about right.
And the not so funny thing is:
I'd be doing the same thing then
as I am now —
missing him.

IHSS is caused by abnormal growth
of the cells in the heart muscle.
In a sense, Brian's heart
grew too big.
I wish that I had gotten the chance
to experience how big Brian's heart
could be.
I wonder what it would have felt like
to have a relationship with Brian
where I wasn't always questioning
and worrying,
and feeling so alone.

It's been six days
since Brian's funeral.
Six days of watching TV,
but never the news.
Six days of sleeping all day
and then not sleeping at night.
Six days of not eating.
Six days of avoiding my mom.
Six days of unanswered
emails, and texts, and voicemails.
The exception was Independence Day,
and that passed quickly.

I'm trying to decide what is worse.
Someone being gone,
but still out there,
or someone being gone forever,
dead.
I think someone being gone,
but still out there, might be worse.
Then there's always the chance,
the hoping,
the wondering
if things might change.
If maybe one day he'll come back.
There's also the wondering about
what his new life is like.
The life without you.
Is he happier?
And if he is,
you're left being sad,
wondering what it would be like
if you were happy with him.

But when someone is dead,
he's dead.
He's not coming back.
There is no second chance.
Death is a period
at the end of a sentence.

Someone gone, but still out there,
is an ellipsis . . . or a question
to be answered.

On the seventh day,
I put on a pair of jean shorts,
a T-shirt, and flip-flops.
I walk out of my house,
turn on my music,
and put the songs on shuffle.
I haven't done this in ages,
but I am ready
for a sign.

There are 318 songs to choose from,
and when I press the PLAY button,
it's like spinning a roulette wheel.
What song will it land on?
What will the message be?
And out of 318 songs,
my message is nothing.
Literally, nothing.
The song that comes up
is instrumental.
That can't be right.
I hit the SKIP button.
The next song is "Little Motel"
by Modest Mouse.
I've never paid attention to the lyrics,
but I suppose I should now.

As I walk toward the cemetery,
I press my earphones farther into my ears
and strain to hear the words.
"I *hope that the suite*
sleeps and suits you well."
That makes me think how people say
when you're dead, you're sleeping.
And I do hope
that Brian is sleeping well.

When the song ends,
I take my headphones off
and walk across the cemetery.
But I don't go right to Brian.
I need to make a stop first.

I sit down on the stone bench,
right on top of the words:
FATHER, INTO THY HANDS
I COMMEND MY SPIRIT
and face Sylvia and Sidney,
Ruth and Herman,
Adele and Morris.

I've been coming to this spot,
talking to them,
for years.

When I was little
I was drawn to their deeply imprinted,
old-fashioned names,
and I would make up stories
about their lives.

Sylvia was a dancer
who performed all over the world.
Sidney was her manager.
One night in Paris,
Sidney confessed his love for her,
and they were married within the month.

Ruth and Herman
were high school sweethearts
who got married at eighteen.
They had five kids of their own,
twice as many grandchildren,
and even more great-grandchildren.
Their house was never quiet,
never empty.

Adele and Morris got married
right before Morris went to war.
He kept her picture in his pocket
and wrote to her every week.
She kept all his letters in a tin

and prayed every night
that he would come back to her.
And he did.

I call them the Dearly Departed,
and have always thought of them
as family.
Instead of telling my mom things,
I would tell them.
I told them when I first got my period,
about crushes on boys,
fights with friends.
I told them anything
I needed to tell.
And they listened,
and never criticized,
and never yelled.

Today, I ask them all for a favor —
something I've never done before.
I say, "Could you please
watch over Brian
and make sure he's okay?
I'm not sure how it all works up there,
but if there's anything you can do,
I would appreciate it.
He's really special."

The dirt on Brian's grave is pretty uneven,
but it looks like someone tried
to pat it down smooth.
I'm sure it was the groundskeepers,
but I can't help imagining
it was Brian's mother —
as if she were tucking him into bed
for the last time.
I look down at the temporary grave marker
and wonder how long it will take
for the real headstone to come.
Brian deserves more than plastic.

I tell Brian what's been going on
as if he doesn't know.
"It's been a week
since your funeral.
The service was packed
with family and friends.
But maybe you already know that.
I didn't talk to your parents,
but I met your grandmother.
She seemed pretty cool."

I pause.

"There are things
I wanted to tell you,

but never did.
So I suppose now
is as good a time as any.
It's not like you can tell me
that you don't want to hear it.

A lot of the time you made me crazy.
I was always wondering
where you were,
what you were doing,
why you weren't calling,
what you were thinking,
if you felt the same way I did.
I wanted to be close to you,
spend more time with you,
for you to share things with me,
but you never did.
But I guess I didn't
tell you everything either.
I never told you
about the Dearly Departed.
About my father.

Even though I liked
that when we were together
we were in this private little bubble,
I wish we had done things

with your friends or mine.
You only met Marissa twice —
both times just for a minute.
And you never even met Joy and Parker.
Sometimes I wonder if I was your secret,
that you thought something about me
was so embarrassing, so awful
that you couldn't bear
to introduce me to your friends."

I pause again and look around.
Brian is next to Lisette Iver.
Her stone says 1903–1997,
that she was a mother,
a grandmother,
and a great-grandmother.
Lisette's husband, Walter,
is on the other side of her.
This cemetery is filled with pairs
or empty plots waiting to receive
people's other halves.
There is so much importance
put on being buried next to loved ones,
so what does it mean
that Brian will not
be next to his family,
that he will never

be buried next to his mate,
that Brian is going to spend eternity
sandwiched between Lisette Iver
and Doug Armstrong?

As I walk home I realize
that I have the answers
to the questions
I've always asked about Brian:

Where is Brian?
    Two blocks away.
What is he doing?
    Lying quietly, still.
When is he going to call?
    Never.

In bed, I cannot sleep.

I think about summer break with my dad.

My dad, Lauren, the twins, and I
go to the beach.
Lauren packs sandwiches and snacks.
My dad packs sunscreen and toys.
As my dad sleeps
and Lauren reads,
Lisa, Sage, and I
build a sand castle.
Over and over,
I dig the plastic shovel
into the wet and gritty sand.
It crunches and scrapes
as it goes in.
When we are done,
there are four towers,
a water-filled moat,
and shells for windows.

Afterward, the twins and I
play in the water.
They run toward the bubbly surf
as a wave rolls in.
But when the water touches their feet,
they run screaming back to their parents,
part in fear

and part in triumph
of what they've just done.

When my dad takes the twins for ice cream,
I put on a fresh coat of SPF,
lie on my stomach,
unhook my top,
and close my eyes.
And the sun makes me sleep
sleep
sleep.

I visit Brian again the next day.
"There are so many things
that we will never get to do.
I will never
take a trip with you.
I will never
dance with you at prom.
I will never
know if we had a future
beyond this summer.
I will never
know if you would have said,
'I love you.'

But there are things
that are much bigger than me.
You will never
graduate high school
or go to college.
You will never
make your friends laugh again.
You will never
go to another concert
and come home with your ears ringing.
You will never
become a successful artist
and sit in Paris or Florence,
sketching people as they go by.

You will never
get married or have kids.
You will never
be hugged again by your parents.
You will never
have your heart broken
and then healed.

There are so many things
you will not get to do.
But what will
you get to do?
Is death the end
or is there more?
Will you watch us from above
and make appearances in our dreams?
Will you rattle the windows
when someone says your name?
Or have you forgotten
us already?"

After talking to Brian,
I walk over to Richardson.
I don't have a destination.
I just start walking
and don't stop.
I pass the pharmacy,
the pizza place,
the nail salon,
the realtor.
And everywhere I look,
there are couples and families.
People are holding hands.
Mothers are carrying babies.
Fathers are pushing strollers.
They all look happy.
And I am alone,
just having come back
from visiting my dead boyfriend.

I have so much tension in my face,
so much tightness,
anger.
I wonder if it's from holding
in the tears
and the screams
that I so badly want to let out,
but don't.

Parker texts me:
I'm calling u in 5 mins.
U better pick up. ;)
When my phone rings,
I reluctantly answer.
He says,
"Lee, you haven't
called me back in days."
    "I know. I haven't felt
    like talking."
"What have you been doing?"
    "Nothing."
"Have you seen anyone?"
    "No."

But that's not true.
I've seen Brian.
But I don't tell Parker that.

He says, "I don't have to work today.
Why don't we do something?
You don't have plans, do you?"
I was going to visit Brian,
but I suppose he'll be there later.
Even though I am silent,
Parker says, "Great! I'll call Joy."

A little while later,
Parker pulls up in front of my house

and honks his car horn.
When I get in, Parker turns back and asks,
"So where should we go?"
When I don't answer, Joy says,
    "There's a new café on Richardson
    with an especially hot barista
    I've been eyeing."
"Done," says Parker.

As we drive out of my neighborhood
and past the cemetery,
I hold my breath.
It's not hard.
This cemetery's only a few blocks long.
I'm not sure why I do it
or where I heard the wives' tale
that if you don't hold your breath,
you'll die young
or not go to heaven.
But it's something I've done
since I was little.
I remember doing it
when my mom and I drove to the city.
There are a few big cemeteries on the way —
some more than a half mile long.
I would hold my breath,
pucker my lips, squint my eyes,
and hold it, hold it, hold it

as long as I could.
Sometimes I made it.
Sometimes I didn't.

There is silence
after we get our coffees.
We all sip and look
at each other over the rims of our cups.
Joy's red hair
is pinned back in an artful
but messy way.
Parker's wearing a new T-shirt
that says THANKS FOR NOTHING.

Parker goes first, telling me
"We don't really know what to say."
    Joy continues, "Lee,
    you must be going through hell."
I take another sip of my latte
and try not to look at them.
It feels like they are leading up to something.
Oh, God.
Is this some sort of intervention?
I've seen shows about that,
and it's never pretty.
That's when Parker reaches into his bag.
"We got this for you."
He slides a book across the little table.

Surviving Loss: A Teen's Guide to Healing
     Joy says, "Maybe it will help.
     Well, not help.
     I mean, it's not going to
     make it stop hurting.
     But maybe it will make it hurt less.
     Shit. I don't know."

I pick up the book
and look at the cover.
It's all blue sky and white clouds
on a beautiful day —
like the day Brian was buried.
"Thanks," I tell them.
And that's all I have.
I don't know
what to say either.

A while ago,
Joy, Parker, and I
had planned to go to an open mic night
with Brian.
It was the first time
they were going to meet him,
and I was as nervous as if Brian
were meeting my mom and dad.
Not that that would ever happen.

I had picked an open mic on purpose.
We could all talk,
but not too much.
The performers would be a buffer.

Around 3:00, I texted Brian:
Parkers getting me at 715.
Will get u after that.
See you later.
But I got no answer.
Maybe Brian didn't think
he needed to respond.
It's not like I had asked a question.

But by 4:30 I was worried.
Had he forgotten?
Was his phone dead?

To distract myself
I took a shower and got dressed.
I had picked my outfit days before:
a fitted green T-shirt with birds on it,
with skinny jeans and flats.
I liked wearing flats with Brian.
Then I'd have to stand on my toes
to kiss him.

I took extra time to do my hair,
putting in the mousse, section by section,
then twisting smaller bits
so the curls would be perfect.
I put on a thick coat of black mascara
to make my green eyes stand out
and then brushed on some shimmery lip gloss
that Joy had given me.

At 5:15, I texted Brian again:
Did u get my txt?

At 6:43, he finally wrote back.
Been out all day.
not gonna make it.
need to chill.

I wanted to explode.
I wanted to break something.
If I hadn't liked my phone so much,
I would have bashed it into pieces.

How was I going to tell Parker and Joy?
They already thought Brian was a flake.
I threw my hair up in a ponytail,
not caring that it would dent the curls
that had taken so long to tame.
It didn't matter now.

When Parker honked for me,
I grabbed my bag and went outside.
When I got in, they both said, "Hey."
Then Parker asked,
"Which way to Brian's house?"
    "He's not coming."
"What?" They both whipped around
and looked at me like angry parents.
"Why not?" asked Joy,
her eyes wide with disbelief.
"He better be dying," said Parker.
I didn't know what to say.
I wanted to lie
and say he was sick,
but I couldn't.
    "He's just not. Okay?
    Let's get there already."
But as far as I was concerned,
the night was already over.

The "death book,"

the one Parker and Joy gave me,
wants me to visualize death as an ocean.
My first thought is that
death would be a sinking ship
and that I would be terrified
as I was being pulled under the water,
away from my mom and my friends.
Or maybe death would be me,
alone
in a rowboat,
on an endlessly calm sea.

But that doesn't seem right either —
especially the part about being alone.
Maybe death is a giant cruise ship
that sails the seas and is inhabited
by everyone who has ever died.
We would play ghost bingo
and have ghost dinners
and stand on the deck
and admire the endless view.

I finally dreamed of Brian.
I was in the park, sitting on a swing.
He came up behind me
and gave me a push.
I turned back to look at him,
waiting for him to say something.
I knew that whatever he said
would be meaningful.
But there was nothing.

He pushed me again, higher.
I looked back.
Still not a word.
Typical Brian.

That's when I realized
the only sound I could hear
was a rhythmic thumping.

Thump. Thump.
Brian pushed me forward.

Thump. Thump.
I swung back.

Thump. Thump.
Brian pushed me forward.

Thump. Thump.
I swung back.

I looked around,
expecting to see someone with a drum,
but I couldn't find the source.
When I turned back to Brian,
I saw that he was shirtless.
His chest had been crudely ripped open,
and blood pulsed
down his stomach in waves.

The sound was coming
from Brian's heart.
He was the source.

I feel
empty
confused
hurt
numb
disoriented
mad
vulnerable
insignificant
blurry
tired
sweaty
overwhelmed
temporary
anxious

It's 3:47 a.m. and I can't sleep.
I can't stop thinking
about something terrible
happening to my mom.

I tiptoe to her room.
The door is open just a little.
She is tangled up in her sheets —
one foot hanging off the bed.
An open book is next to her face.
She snores softly.

Without her,
I would be lost.
And furiously regretful
for not
spending more time with her.
For not
really talking to her.

I lean against the door frame.
I want to wake her up and tell her
about Brian.
I want to tell her lots of things.
But I can't.
I always stop myself.
Maybe because it doesn't feel safe.

Like if I tell her anything,
it will open me up
to having to answer all her questions.

After sitting with Brian this afternoon,
I walk along the very last row of graves.
It's so deep in the shade
that only moss grows here.
Most of the gravestones are buried
under dirt,
so only part of the story
can be read.
Some of the gravestones creep
out of the ground only a few inches —
determined to remind us
that they are still here.
All that's left to see are the words
FATHER or IN MEMORY OF.
I wonder what happened.
I wonder what made the earth rise up.

I don't

want to do anything.
I don't
have the energy to do anything
besides watch TV,
read, and visit Brian.
I don't
want to talk to my friends.
Being alone somehow seems safer.
I don't
want to go back to school in the fall.
I don't
know how I'll be able to sit still in class,
learning useless crap like calculus.
I don't
want to apply to college.
I am changed.
My perspective is changed.
I don't
think I can come back from that.
I don't
think I can live the way I did before.
Not thinking
about all the terrible things that can happen.
Not knowing
what it feels like
to have a part of me ripped out.
How do I come back from this?

It's not always easy
to get in to see Brian.
Sometimes when I go to the cemetery,
there's already a person there.
So I stand with the Dearly Departed
or in front
of a stranger's grave
and wait
and watch.

I saw Brian's mom there once.
She was holding a bunch of sunflowers.
Even from a distance
I could see that she was talking to him.
I wondered what she was saying.
Did she tell Brian how much she missed him?
How her life would never be the same?
Or maybe she wasn't talking to Brian,
but to God, telling him how she was furious
for taking away her only child.
Who knows, maybe she was praying,
offering God her unwavering trust.

I've also seen several people my age.
The guys seem to come alone.
The girls in pairs.
Some cry.
Some bring flowers.

Some stand there
for a few moments,
then walk away.

When I see someone at Brian's grave,
I am torn.
I want to go over.
I want someone to grieve with,
to share stories with.
But I also want to avoid
explaining who I am,
what Brian was to me,
and most of all
the inevitable
lack of recognition on their faces.
I suppose I could just say we were friends
and leave it at that,
but that doesn't feel right either.

I'm not sure I understand the point,
or the higher purpose,
or if there was any purpose at all.
Did God have a master plan?
And if so,
how could taking Brian away
possibly fit into it?
I don't want to hear bullshit excuses like:
"God took Brian
because he wanted Brian near him."
What was gained
by taking Brian away?
I can only see grief.
I can only see pain.

Why did Brian only get a partial life?
Why do I get to live when he doesn't?
It doesn't make sense.
It makes me furious.
It makes me think there is no God.

Maybe if Brian had known
how short his life was going to be,
he could have lived it more fully.
If I could ask Brian
what he would have done differently
in his short life,
what would he say?

I wonder if I can somehow
make it through all this
without actually living it —
curl up in a dark cave
and sleep, belly full,
like a bear
until springtime.

Things feel different.
It's hard to explain,
but all this has shocked me.
I feel like I have electricity
running through me,
like I have been turned on
in a way that I wasn't before.
I am so much more aware
that I am a person,
my own person.
And that makes me feel big,
but it also makes me feel small.
There are billions of people in this world,
and we are all alive and buzzing and thinking
that we are the center of the universe.
And we are so far from it.
Just thinking of how I figure
into the vastness of space
scares me.
It makes me feel insignificant
and that me mourning Brian is nothing,
not even a flicker in this world.
And even though I know
that this life is tiny,
it's all I've got.
It's my life.
It's my universe.

Sitting and talking to Brian

is exhausting,
since I have to do all the talking.
I wish I could get a sign from him
that he's listening.
It'd be nice to know he's there.
I wonder how a sign
might look or sound.
Maybe a breeze would blow by,
and I would get a whiff of his cologne.
Or maybe a bird would land on Brian's grave
and start chirping at me.
Maybe a leaf would fall out of the trees
and land in the palm of my hand.
I close my eyes
and wait, quietly.
I take a long deep breath in
and just when I am about to exhale,
a car backfires.
It's gunshot-loud.
That sign
is loud and clear.

Joy calls.
She wants to know
if I want to go shopping.
I say no.

Parker calls.
He wants to know
if I want to go to the movies.
I say no.

Marissa calls.
She wants to know
if I want to go for lunch.
I say no.

At 6:30 p.m., my mom comes downstairs,
dressed and ready for the night shift.
I am in my pajamas and on the couch
watching an Iron Chef marathon.
"All right, I'm off to the hospital.
There's lasagna in the freezer.
If you decide to go out with friends tonight,
just leave me a voicemail, okay?"

"Sure," I answer,
knowing I'm not going anywhere.
"I'll see you tomorrow morning.
Have a good night."

As I watch episode after episode,
the hours slip by.
The only time I move
is to refill my cereal bowl
or go to the bathroom.
And even that takes effort.

Somewhere around 2:00 a.m.,
I pull the blanket over my head,
turn my back to the TV,
and fall asleep.
I don't even bother
to turn off the lights or the TV.
Motivating to go upstairs to my room
is completely out of the question.

The sound of the front door shutting
wakes me around 7:30 a.m.
"What are you still doing down here?"
my mom asks as she puts down her bag.

"I guess I fell asleep while watching TV."
I push back the blanket and rub my eyes.
"I'm judging from your pj's
that you didn't go out last night."

"I wasn't in the mood,"
I say as I stand up
and head for the stairs.
All I want
is to be in my bed.
"You've been staying in a lot.
Is something wrong?
Are you not feeling well?"

"I'm fine.
Just tired."
"All right, well, maybe
we can do something later.
Want to come get a manicure?"

"Maybe.
Let's talk after you wake up."
But I have no intention of being around
when she wakes up.
I'm spending the afternoon with Brian.

The next week,
Parker invites me to Great Adventure.
I say no thank you.

Joy invites me to the flea market.
I say no thank you.

Marissa invites me to the beach.
I say no thank you.

The death book wants me
to look in the mirror.
It wants to know what I see.
I see bad skin.
I see circles under my eyes.
I see eyebrows that need to be plucked,
pimples that need to be popped,
curls that are dry and knotted.
I see lips that don't want to smile.
I see tired, cloudy eyes —
eyes that don't want to cry anymore.

Staring into my eyes
is hypnotizing me.
But instead of bringing me calm,
it makes me feel a pain in my chest.
I am looking at a stranger.

I wonder how it would look
if someone took an X-ray
of the ground at the cemetery.
Maybe it would look like
a scene from a beach —
dozens of bodies, stretched out
trying to get some sun.

Marissa stops by unannounced.
When I let her in, she says,
"Hey, I don't have to babysit today,
so I thought I'd come over
and see what's going on."

But nothing is going on.
I am sitting on the couch in my pj's,
watching daytime talk shows.

"God, it's so hot in here.
Don't you have the AC on?"
   "I didn't feel like getting up
   to turn it on."
Marissa walks over to the AC
and puts it on HIGH.

She sits down next to me and asks,
"What are you watching?"
   "Oprah. Why men cheat."
"Sounds exciting.
Why don't we go for a walk?"
   "Nah. I'm tired."
"Tired from watching Oprah?"
   "Nah. Just tired in general."
"Come on. It's beautiful out."
   "No thanks.
   I'm just gonna hang here."

Marissa gets up.
It looks like she's going to leave.
I'm glad.
I don't want to talk
to anyone.
But then she suddenly turns back.
"Brian died, not you, Annaleah.
Your life can't stop
just because his did."
Her words take my breath away.

After a moment I say,
"You have no idea
what you're talking about."
"Well, then tell me."
"Tell you what?"
"Tell me how it is for you.
You don't talk to me.
You don't call me back.
All you do is sit at the cemetery."
"What? Have you been stalking me?"
"No, Annaleah.
I've just seen you there a few times
during my walks with Dana and Steven.
I don't get it.
We stopped talking because of Brian.
And now that's he's gone,
we're still not talking.

It doesn't make any sense.
I thought that after the funeral,
things would change."

"Things *have* changed."
"Yeah.
I can see that."

This time she leaves for real,
slamming the screen door behind her.

I stare out the window
and watch her walk down the street.
Once Marissa's out of sight,
I go upstairs and get dressed.
I need to tell Brian about this.

I wear my favorite sundress,
the one with the blue flowers
and straps that tie at the shoulders
to visit Brian today.
I even pack lunch.
Brian and I never went on a picnic
so I figure, why not now?

I spread out a small blanket next to him
and take out an apple.
In between chews I say,
"I was reading this book last night
about death and different cultures.
One part talked about how
Hopis use feathers in burials.
I would have liked
to do what they do —
cover you in soft white feathers,
lay them over your eyes and mouth,
and put them on your hands and feet.
That way you could float away,
get wherever you were going quickly,
smoothly.

Oh! And there's a place
in central Asia called Turkistan,
not that I'd ever heard of it before,
where they dig L-shaped graves.

They lower the body down
and then slip it into a nook on the side.
That way when the grave is filled in,
no dirt falls on the body.
I think it's kind of nice.
Gentle.
Respectful."

I stop.
"Maybe you don't want
to hear about this."

I think for a moment
and then reach into my bag.
I tear off a bit of my sandwich.
"If a bird or squirrel eats this bread
in less than fifteen seconds,
then you want to hear more.
If nothing tries to eat it,
then you want me to stop."

I toss the crust several feet away
into the grass and count,
"One, two, three, four,
five, six, seven, eight . . ."
Two little brown birds
hop toward the bread.
"Nine, ten, eleven . . ."

The first bird grabs one end of the crust,
the second nibbles the other side.
I smile a little smile.

"Javanese Muslims
do this washing ceremony thing.
They cradle the body on their laps
as if it were a child.
Then they wash the body while holding it,
and get soaked in the process.
The book called it
'a last demonstration of nurturing love.'
It sounds so beautiful.
So personal.
So intimate.
I wonder who washed you."

In bed, I cannot sleep.
I think about my dad
at my middle school graduation.

He sits toward the front,
right next to my mom.
And even though
it's hard for them,
they don't fight.

From up on the stage,
I can see my dad
holding a huge bouquet.
Daisies.
Nothing but dozens of daisies.
He remembered.

When my name is called
and I cross the stage,
I hear a chorus
of cheering and clapping.
I know the loudest of those
is my father.

Afterward, my dad and I
go for lunch.
Just the two of us.
The sky has turned gray.

The air in the car is heavy
with humidity
and the crisp smell of daisies.
As the rain tap-taps
against the windshield
and the windshield wipers
swipe-swipe back and forth,
I lean my head against the window
and sleep
sleep
sleep.

There is a pain
under my left rib.
I wonder if it's because
my belly is empty.
Or maybe it's because
all of me is empty.
My tear ducts are empty.
I can't imagine that I will ever
have any more tears to cry.
My heart is empty.
But my brain —
my brain is full.
It races with thoughts
of what could have been.

The death book taught me

two new words today:
columbarium and *mausoleum*.
The first is a resting place
for someone's ashes.
The second is an aboveground
burial structure.
These words seem
old and mysterious.
And maybe also
a little beautiful too.

Sitting with Brian is too quiet.
I take out my music and put it on shuffle
to get a message.
"Idioteque" by Radiohead comes up.
The song is fast, frantic.
It makes my heart race
in an uncomfortable way.
And the message is not clear.

"Here I'm alive.
Everything all of the time."

Is that supposed to mean
that Brian's soul is alive in heaven,
that he can still take everything in?
Or is he talking about
how I am left here,
alive without him,
and feeling everything —
every painful moment?

"You can't just lie here all day,"
my mom says
while standing in my doorway.
She is holding her purse in one hand
and her car keys in the other.
I stare at her from my bed, thinking,
Sure I can.
I've been doing it
for the last few weeks.

"Why don't you come to the mall?"
     "You think going to the mall
     is better than staying here?"
"Yes. Get dressed.
I'll wait for you downstairs."
This time it isn't a question.
It's a statement.
And I don't have the energy to fight,
so I twist my hair into a bun
and root around on the floor
for reasonably clean shorts,
a tank top, and a pair of sneakers.
Washing my face is out of the question.
The most I can manage is deodorant.

My mom does most of the talking in the car.
She tells me what's been happening
with the other nurses at work.

There's always some dirty bit of gossip
passing through those sanitized halls.
Usually, it's entertaining,
but today I'm barely listening.
I'm planning my escape.

"What's going on
with Marissa, Joy, and Parker?"
she asks, changing the subject.
I don't have an answer.
I haven't seen any of them in a while.
The only thing I can tell her with certainty
is that a few blades of grass
have sprouted on Brian's grave.
        "Don't know.
        They've all been really busy.
        Parker's got an internship
        at an ad agency in the city.
        Joy's working at a boutique.
        And Marissa's nannying."
"Busy."
    She pauses and shakes her head.
"That's what you should be."

The mall is awful.
There's no way
fighting with my mom
about staying home

would have been worse than this.
It's loud, crowded, too bright,
smells of greasy food.
And it's freezing.
It's almost August.
I shouldn't need a sweater.

I follow my mom from store to store
as she does her errands:
new dress,
overpriced skin cream,
linen tablecloth.
When she's done she asks,
"Do you want to go to Victoria's Secret?
I saw your bras and panties in the wash.
You could use some fresh ones."
Hearing her say "panties" is torture.
And what do I need new underwear for?
I don't care if they're dingy
and unraveling.
It's not like anyone's looking.
    "It's okay. Thanks."
"Are you sure?
It's my treat."
    "Yeah. I'm sure."
"Do you want to stop in anywhere else?
Maybe some new skirts and tops?

Or a pair of pretty sandals?" she asks,
glancing at my less than impressive outfit.
    "No, I'm sure. Thanks.
    Can we just go?
    There's a yoga class I want to get to."
"Oh, how nice! Good for you!"
She is way too excited,
which makes me feel bad
because I'm not really going to yoga.
I'm going to visit Brian.

I am thankful that Brian

is buried near my house.
It keeps us close.
Slows the separation.
Just like the poem
Peter read at the funeral:

I am but waiting for you for an interval
Somewhere very near
Just around the corner.

I read in the death book
that the Yuqui, in South America,
don't bury their dead.
They leave the body to decompose
and then clean and paint the skull red.
Next the skull is given to a close relative,
who carries it with him during the day
and keeps it under his hammock at night.
When the skull starts to disintegrate,
it is discarded.
The book says that now
"the duty of honoring the deceased
has been fulfilled."
This seems so loving.
Keeping the person with you —
even if it's just his bones.

I'm telling Brian

about shopping with my mom,
when I hear someone come up behind me.
I turn around to see who it is,
then quickly stand up.
It's Brian's grandmother.
The one I met at the funeral.

"Oh, I can go,"
I say, picking up my bag.
    "Now, why would you do that?
    There's no reason we can't visit together."
"Okay. Thanks."
    "We met at the funeral,
    didn't we?"
"Yes. I'm Annaleah."
    "Hmmm. Annaleah.
    What a beautiful name."
She pauses for a bit
to stare at Brian's grave,
then starts again,
    "When Brian was little,
    he never stopped moving.
    Helene, my daughter-in-law,
    said she couldn't get any sleep
    while she was pregnant with him.
    He just wouldn't stop moving around.

Even as a child, when he slept,
Brian was always twitching
or kicking free of the covers.
And now,
he's at rest.
Hard to imagine."

I'd never heard a story about Brian as a child.
It makes me smile to imagine him, little,
running around like crazy.
A blur in the room.
"What will you remember most
about Brian?" his grandmother asks.
Images flash through my mind.
Brian laughing.
Brian drawing.
Brian leaning in to kiss me.
"I don't know.
There are a lot of things."
"He was really special.
But you already knew that."
She looks right at me.
There are those Dennis blue eyes again.

Maybe Brian told her about us.
Or maybe she senses it.
But it doesn't really matter right now.

What matters
is that for the first time
since Brian was buried,
I am not standing here alone.

I have cornflakes.

My mom has eggs and toast.

We maneuver around each other.

She reaches for the salt.

I reach for the sugar.

She reaches for the pepper.

I reach for a napkin.

No words.

No touching.

Barely even eye contact.

I have nothing to say,

but I can feel

that she's building toward something.

"Did you get into a fight with your friends?"

I look back at her with squinted eyes.

    "What? No.

    They're just busy with work."

"You know, I could get you

a volunteer position at the hospital,"

she says gently.

"We always need a hand

with delivering flowers, making copies,

or walking patients to appointments.

A job like that would look great

on your college applications."

    "Thanks, but I don't think so.

    I've got a lot going on."

"Like what?" she snaps.
"You don't do anything."
     "I do plenty,"
     I say, pushing back my chair.
I put my bowl in the sink
and go to my room
to get dressed to visit Brian.
I do
plenty.

What would it be like if I had died
instead of Brian?
Would the whole school have turned out
and appeared brokenhearted —
even the girls who talk trash about me?
What would it have been like
to have all those people in my house?
Friends, family, teachers, acquaintances,
maybe even some strangers.
Something would be missing
and that something
would be me.
It'd be like not inviting the guest of honor
to her own party.

And my mom,
my mom,
my mom.
How would it have been for her,
with no husband's shoulder to cry on,
no parents of her own to give her comfort?

Who would have spoken at my funeral?
What would people have said?
Would my mom have been able to find the words?
Would my dad have shown up?

Maybe one of my teachers would have spoken.
But which one?

Definitely not Mr. Lowry.
He was giving me Ds in history.
I don't think someone who gave you Ds
would speak at your funeral.
Although he always said
that I had great potential —
just that I wasn't working up to it.
Maybe he would have said something about that.

Ms. Lohman would be the likely one.
I got As in creative writing.
She said I had a vivid imagination
and a talent for creating characters and stories.
Maybe she would have said something about that.

Maybe Joy and Parker
would have read a poem.
They're always doing dramatic things like that.
But I hope it wouldn't have been that poem about God,
and footsteps, and being carried.
Because that's bullshit.

I hope Marissa would have spoken.
Maybe she would've told some funny stories
from when we were kids.
Maybe she would've said she was sorry
for how things have been with us lately.

And Brian?
What about Brian?
Would he be going through
the same things I am now?

I walk down my block
and then take a right turn.
Two more blocks
and I'll be with Brian.
For the first time
in a long time,
I know he'll be there
waiting for me.

I sit down on the grass next to him.
He has flowers,
but I know they're not for me.
I wonder who gave them to him,
but I don't ask.

I tell Brian about my day.
I say, "I saw your dad
at the supermarket.
I didn't talk to him —
it's not like he knows who I am,
and even if he did,
I wouldn't know what to say.

I watched him
take things off the shelves,
look them over,
and then put them back.
There was almost nothing

in his cart.
I wonder if he's always been like that,
or just lately."
I say, "I miss you."
I ask if he's missed me too,
then wait for his answer.

If that squirrel runs up that tree,
then his answer is yes.
If it stays on the grass,
his answer is no.

The squirrel doesn't move,
and my breath catches in my throat.
After a moment,
it zips up the tree.
I smile and lie down
next to Brian.
I wish he could hold me
like he used to,
but he doesn't.

The warm sun makes me drowsy
and I fall asleep on my side
next to Brian.
When I wake up, grass is imprinted
on my arm and leg.
I brush myself off,

but Brian doesn't move.
I say, "I'll see you tomorrow."
I reach out to touch him,
and my fingers make contact
with words:

BRIAN DENNIS
DIED AGE SEVENTEEN
BELOVED SON AND FRIEND

I had a dream

that I was being buried.
Not buried alive exactly,
but buried
with a consciousness.
And I could see everything
happening aboveground.

I saw
the dirt being shoveled on top of me.
I saw
it being patted down smooth.
I saw
the mourners leave one by one.
Each time someone else left,
I cried out,
"Don't leave me.
Don't leave me here alone.
I don't want to be
left alone
for forever."
But there was no sound.
No words.

Sitting on the bench
across from the Dearly Departed,
I prop my elbows on my thighs
and put my chin in my hands.
I stare down at the ground.
Moss, grass, clovers.
Then I look up the hill
and survey the scene.
All the names and dates
on the graves are facing me.
Like faces looking into mine,
poised, ready to talk.

I can see my reflection
in one of the polished gravestones.
It's blurry,
but it's there.
When the sun goes behind a cloud,
I disappear.

The death book wants me

to write down everything I remember
about Brian —
all the small details.

I remember how
his dark eyelashes made his eyes seem so light
he always carried his sketchbook
he had a freckle right at the corner of his lips
he wore jeans that were a little too big
he always smelled like soap
he liked to quote from movies
his favorite sweatshirt had a hole in the side
he sometimes had a book in his back pocket
the hair on his arms was surprisingly soft
he thought Family Guy was the best thing ever
he made fun of me for watching reality TV
his nails were usually ragged
he put at least three packets of sugar in his coffee
he never seemed to wear matching socks
he was obsessed with Stanley Kubrick
he was always hungry
his teeth were perfectly straight
he was squeamish about reptiles
he got the chills whenever I kissed his ears

Fireflies blink

Morse code messages from Brian.
Crickets chirp
notes that when read on a scale
surely have meaning.
Unfortunately, I don't speak
their language.

All this thinking about death
can't be good for me.
I liked it better when I was
unaware of how my days are numbered.
That one day, maybe soon,
all of this will just stop.
It makes me wonder
about my life
and what I'm doing with it.
What will I do?
What will I never do?
Will I ever see the Egyptian pyramids?
I suppose that's up to me,
but if I don't see them now —
in this life —
I will never see them.

And what about school?
I'm stuck in school for one more year.
That will make fourteen years in total
of learning what someone else
has decided is important
so I can take some bullshit tests
that will decide what kind of education
I am worthy of.
Then it's four more years of school
that are supposed to prepare me for a career —
one that is pretty much a mystery to me.

And what about Brian?
What did all his education get him?
How did knowing algebra help him?
Brian would have been better off
traveling the world rather than memorizing
information in textbooks.

As I am walking past the church
on my way to the cemetery,
I see Brian's dad getting out of his car.
I stop.
I stare.
If he's going to visit Brian,
I should come back later.
Give them some time
together.

But he doesn't walk into the cemetery.
He walks toward the church doors,
which have a group of people around them.

I wonder what could be happening
at church at 7:00 p.m. on a Sunday night.
Maybe it's a service for Brian.
But why wouldn't his mom be with his dad?
And where are all the people my age?
There are only adults.
That's when I notice the hand-painted sign
on the church's double doors.
AA

When I get to Brian I say,
"Why didn't you ever tell me?
Did you even know?
Or did you know

and just not want to tell?
Maybe that's something else
we had in common —
not telling the truth
about our dads."

I take a deep breath and sit down.
My anger subsides.

After about an hour
of listening to my music on shuffle
and talking to Brian,
people begin filing out of the church.
That's my signal
to leave Brian's grave
and go back near the church doors.
I want to get a better look at Mr. Dennis.
Maybe even hear his voice.

Eventually, Brian's dad comes out,
shakes some hands,
and gets some pats on the back.
Then, hands in his jeans pockets,
he walks into the cemetery.

I wish I could hear
what he is saying to Brian.
Or know what he is thinking.

I wish I could know their family stories,
see the insides of their photo albums.
I wish I could make new memories with them,
and that one day I could have been invited
for Christmas or Thanksgiving.
But that's never going to happen now.
The best I can do
is come back next Sunday night
and see if his dad is here again.
Maybe I'll work up the courage
to talk to him then.

I don't have to wait
a week to see Brian's dad again.
He's at the deli a few nights later.
I'm buying a box of donuts,
and he's at the counter ordering sandwiches.

Seeing him must be a coincidence,
but then I wonder
if it's some kind of sign from Brian.
Maybe his dad has a message for me.
Maybe I have one for him
and don't even know it.

I am desperate to hear Mr. Dennis's voice.
But more so,
to hear his voice
directed to me.

But what I would say?
Maybe, "Hello,
I was a friend of Brian's,
and I am sorry for your loss."
That hardly seems appropriate
while standing in front of sliced meats.
But is there really ever a good place or time
to express grief?

When Mr. Dennis pays and walks by me,
I get lost in his eyes —
Brian's eyes.
I am frozen.
My mouth hangs open a little.
I say nothing.

In bed, I cannot sleep.
I think about Christmas
with my dad in LA.

Piles of presents are positioned
underneath a massive sparkling tree.
Lisa and Sage are running around the house,
high on sugar, draped in garlands.

My father keeps hugging me.
He kisses my forehead,
tells me how much I've grown
since the summer.
He asks how school is
and how dating is going.
I tell him school sucks
and that it's gross
to talk to your dad about dating.
But he insists, tells me
that anyone who is important to me
is important to him.
But there isn't anyone important
yet.

That night,
Lauren cooks a Christmas feast,
and after we eat, all five of us

squeeze onto the couch.
We watch *Rudolph* on DVD
and then sleep
sleep
sleep.

Lewis Armin

died on April 10, 1877.

He was 41.

Sarah Armin

died on July 27, 1896.

She was 68.

I suppose they were

husband and wife.

But they could have been

brother and sister.

The bottom of their stone says:

GONE BUT NOT FORGOTTEN

Maybe that was true in 1896

and for a while after.

But is that true now,

more than one hundred years later?

Is there anyone left

who remembers them?

Who will visit Brian

in one hundred years?

Who will remember him then?

Who will remember me?

What's the point of having all this

if you are forgotten?

The death book wants me
to make a Question Jar.
It says to write down my questions,
put them in the jar,
and then let them go.
It tells me that this is not
about finding answers.
That it's just about
the process of asking.

I pull a glass jar out of the recycling bin,
rinse it out, and then dry it off.
Next I take a piece of paper
and rip it into small strips.
Then I start writing.

Why did this happen?
I crumple it up and toss it in the jar.

Is there a heaven?
I crumple it up and toss it in the jar.

When will it not hurt like this?
I crumple it up and toss it in the jar.

Did Brian actually care about me?
I crumple it up and toss it in the jar.

Can Brian hear me when I talk to him?
I crumple it up and toss it in the jar.

I still feel like shit.

I'm getting sick

of hearing my own voice.
I need a sign.
Something from Brian
telling me what to do.

I position myself so I am
facing Brian squarely.
I sit up straight,
cross my legs like in yoga,
rest my upturned palms on my knees,
and I wait
and wait.
I wait
for another car to backfire,
for a butterfly to fly by,
for a bee to sting me,
for something.
Anything.
And I wait
and I wait
and I wait.
There is nothing
except the sound
of birds and cars.

I stand up and grab my stuff.
I am so mad
I can't even look at Brian.

At home I am as furious

as if Brian and I
had gotten into a fight.
I throw my bag on my desk,
and it knocks into a stack of college catalogs.
As they spill onto the floor,
a menu from Renzo's, covered in doodles,
falls too.
From across the room
I recognize the drawings.
I dive for it
as if some great gust of wind
might rip through my bedroom
and blow it away forever.

My mouth goes dry.
I trace my finger over the ink lines
as if tracing the veins in Brian's arm.
This drawing isn't new.
It isn't from beyond the grave.
Brian was doodling on this menu
while he was in my room one afternoon.
But it can't be a coincidence
that I am finding this now.
This is definitely my sign.

Part Three

I walk through the door at Renzo's.

I'm not sure
what I am supposed to be doing
or what I am supposed to be looking for.
So I just stand there,
by the counter.
Every time the door opens behind me,
I turn to see who it is.
My heart hopes
that Brian will walk through that door
and tell me that all this has been a mistake.
But I know that's not going to happen.
So I wait
and stare.

After a few minutes a voice breaks my trance.
"Can I help you?"
asks a guy from behind the counter.
Annoyed that he has disrupted my thoughts,
I just shake my head.
I need to keep looking for signs.

But he starts talking again,
"'Cause, you know,
if you like standing around here so much,
you should apply for the waitress job."
I don't even process what he's said.
He is a car honking in the background.

He is an annoying person talking during a movie.
He is a mosquito buzzing in my ear.
I try to focus,
keeping an eye out for signs.
They could come in any form.
"It could be the change
you're looking for," he says.
That snaps me to attention.
For the first time since I came in,
I really look at him.
He's tall and thin,
and maybe a little older than me.
He's got light hair and brown eyes,
and a glob of pizza sauce on his shirt.
    "A change?" I ask.
"Yeah," he says.
"Working a few days a week,
making some extra money,
and, of course, all the pizza you can eat."
    "A change?" I ask again.
But this time
I am saying it to myself
and not to him.

The next morning,
I show my mom the job application.
"A pizza place?" she asks skeptically.
"I'm glad you decided to get a job,
but wouldn't you rather work at a clothing store?
What about the boutique Joy's working at?
Or babysitting like Marissa?"
    "No. I have this feeling
    that working at Renzo's is gonna be good."
"A feeling?
Well, if this is what you want . . .
then I think it's great."

I go up to my room
and fill out the application.
The top half is easy.
I write in my name,
address, birthday,
social security number,
and school info.

The bottom half is harder:
work experience and skills.
I don't really have either.
I've babysat,
but I don't think that counts.
So under skills I just write:
I'm really good at math.

I'm a little nervous.
I've never done anything
like this before.
In fact, I haven't done anything
in a long time.

On the way to Renzo's,
I pass the cemetery.
I don't stop to see Brian,
but do nod in his direction.
I'll be back later.

Pizza Boy is behind the counter again.

"You're back," he says.

"Yeah. I filled out the application."

He takes it from me and looks it over.

"Annaleah. Nice name.

Looks like you're good at math, Annaleah."

It's a little weird

how he keeps repeating my name.

He says,

"Let me pass this to my boss."

Pizza Boy comes out from behind the counter

and heads for the kitchen.

He comes back with an older man and says,

"Frank, this is my friend Annaleah.

I think she'd be great

at working the back tables."

Friend? I only met him yesterday.

I don't even know his name.

Frank looks me and my application over.

"Ever waitressed before?" he asks.

I attempt a joke,

"No, but I clear the table at home."

"See, Frank. She's funny.

Customers will like her," says Pizza Boy.

"Do you think you can carry the trays?"

Frank asks, pointing to a tray

that's loaded with dirty plates and cups.

"Definitely," I say,
even though I'm not so sure.
"Okay, then," Frank says.
"Can you do a mix
of afternoon and evening shifts
until school starts?
Then maybe some weekends
after September?"

"Yes. Thank you," I answer,
wondering what Brian's gotten me into.
"All right, then.
You start in two days.
Come in at four.
Wear black pants and a white polo shirt.
See you then."
He shakes my hand
and then goes back to the kitchen.
But Pizza Boy is still standing there.

"Thanks for doing that," I say.

"Telling him you know me, I mean."
"No problem."

"I guess now would be a good time
for you to tell me your name . . .
since we're *friends* and all."
"It's Ethan."

"Well, Ethan.
See you in two days."

"So I went to Renzo's,"
I tell Brian later that afternoon.
"At first, I wasn't sure
why you sent me there.
But then that guy asked me
if I was there about the job
and it all clicked.

But visiting you,
talking to you,
has kept you close.
Feeling sad
has kept me busy —
it's been my job.
And if I come here less,
what will I have?

But I am going to try,
because this
is what you want."

Ethan is behind the counter

when I get to Renzo's
for my first day of work.
"Hey," I say.
Ethan tosses me an order pad
and an apron
to tie around my waist.
    "Frank's not here yet.
    So I'm going to show you around.
    This is Lou," he says.
He's pointing to a chubby guy
who nods in my direction.
    "Lou's usually on the ovens with me.
    Come on, I'll introduce you
    to the cooks in back."
Ethan leads me into the back
and through old saloon-type doors.
    "Mike, Frank, Jimmy,
    this is Annaleah.
    She's the new waitress."
They all smile and wave at me
from behind columns of steam
and piles of chopped vegetables.
I push out a smile
and wave back.
Smiling is new.
For the last few weeks,
none of the muscles in my face

have been put to much use.
No smiles.
No frowns.
No eyebrows raised.
No wrinkled brow.
No nothing.
It all hung there
on the bone —
motionless.

Ethan grabs a menu
and we sit down in one of the booths.
"If someone orders
pizza or calzones and stuff like that,
let us know up front.
If it's kitchen stuff
like salad, meat, and pasta,
let the guys know in the back."
Ethan points to the menu and says,
"If someone orders from this side of the menu,
they get a salad to start
and steamed vegetable of the day."
He goes on to list
more dressings than I can remember at once,
to explain how each booth has a number,
and that as soon as someone sits down,
I should give them a breadbasket
and take their drink orders.

"You getting all this?" he asks.

"Yeah," I say as I try to repeat
all those dressings in my head.

"Ribbit."

"Excuse me?" I ask, totally confused.

"R-I-B-B-T.
Ranch, Italian, blue cheese, balsamic, thousand island.
It'll help you remember."

"Pretty clever, thanks."

"No problem.
So, if it's quiet, you can refill
the salt, pepper, and sugar.
You can also make napkin wraps
or just hang out with me and Lou.
All right, Annaleah,
that's pretty much the end of your tutorial."

As Ethan walks back up front,
he looks over his shoulder and says,
"If you need anything,
I'm here."

The answer to the question
of how many slices of pizza
it takes to make me feel really sick:
three and a half.

I am sweeping
bits of crust, straws,
gum wrappers,
and shredded napkins
into piles,
into a dustpan,
and into the garbage can.
I want to do the same
with my feelings.
I want to sweep them together
into neat piles,
then toss them out.
I want them
away from me.

I sit with Brian and tell him about work.

"At Renzo's, I'm just a waitress.

I'm not the girl

whose quasi-boyfriend died.

To Ethan,

to Lou,

to the customers,

I'm just a regular girl.

No one asks questions like:

Are you okay?

Why don't you call me back?

How do you feel?

Did you eat today?

Did you sleep last night?

The only questions I get are:

Can I get some more bread?

Do you have root beer?

Does this have anchovies?

But when I leave work,

I go back to being me.

To being sad.

To visiting you."

I'm wiping down table six

when I turn around and see Marissa
and Jessica Bennett giving Ethan
their order at the front counter.
This is the first time I've seen Marissa
since she stormed out of my house.

"What are you doing here?"
she asks, walking toward me.

"I started working here a few days ago."
"Oh," she says.
She looks wounded
that I didn't tell her earlier.

"It happened kind of quick."
"Well . . . how are you?"

"Okay, I guess.
I needed to get out of the house,
you know."

But maybe that isn't the right thing to say.
Marissa's been trying to get me
out of the house since Brian died,
and I haven't been willing.
Marissa looks back toward the counter.
"So . . . Jess is waiting.
I should —"

"Yeah.
I've gotta get back to work."

But that's not true.
It's quiet enough that I could talk to her.

If I wanted to.
If she wanted to.
If it weren't so weird.

While Marissa and Jessica
wait up front for their orders,
I check on my tables,
refill some waters,
get someone a straw.
Marissa is only a few yards away,
but she's never felt so far.

Seeing Marissa's shock
makes me think I should
tell Parker and Joy
about getting a job.

I don't want to talk,
so I send a text instead.
Got job @ renzos pizza
on richardson & park.
Come visit if u want.

Joy texts back immediately.
OMG! Thurs?
Im gonna make u work
4 yr tip! ☺

Parker texts the next day.
Waitress? For reals?
Will try to come by soon.

On the way to work,
I see a dead bird
lying on the sidewalk.
It isn't a translucent chick,
fallen from its nest.
It isn't flattened
from the impact of a car.
It is perfect.
Yellow and brown,
with waxy feathers,
a full round body,
and an open eye
looking right at me.

I wonder where this bird came from.
I wonder how it got here.
It's not even near a tree.
I wonder how it died.
It looks as if it
were flying one moment.
Then the next,
struck down from the sky,
dead.

I dream

my cell phone rings.
Marissa is calling.
She tells me
my mother is dead.
Suddenly, Marissa
is in my room.
Her arms and legs
are wrapped around me.
She is holding me.
Rocking me.
She is my skin.
If she lets go,
my body will fall apart.

"Who's that guy?" Joy asks

as she sits down in a booth.

"What guy?"

"The tall one behind the counter."

"Oh. That's Ethan."

"He's hot," she says as she adjusts
the absurdly large silk flower in her hair.

"I guess."

"You don't think so?"

I lean back
and take a good look at Ethan.

"Yeah. I guess he's cute."

"What's his deal?"

"I don't know.
He just finished his first year
at Woodson."

"Does he have a girlfriend?"

"I don't know.
I don't think so.
He hasn't mentioned anyone."

"You should totally go out with him.
He's looked over here
like a million times."

"I don't think so."

"Why not?"

I pause.

"Because of Brian."

Now Joy pauses.

"Really? But Brian —"
    "I better get your pizza,"
    I say as I get up.
I don't need her
to finish her sentence.
I don't need her
to remind me
what Brian and I were
or weren't.

"I wonder
how long grief lasts.
Will there be a day
when I don't feel like this?
When I don't think about you?
I wonder
how long that will be from now.
Weeks?
Months?
Years?
Will I be thirty and still miss you?
Will I always wonder
what our life
could have been?

Maybe we would have
only lasted another few weeks.
Maybe I would have
gotten angry enough
to demand that I be
your actual girlfriend.
Or maybe you would have
ended things with me,
found someone else
you'd rather be with.
There are so many endings
that our story could have had.

But I will never know
any ending besides this one."

The death book wants me

to create an obituary for Brian.
It says to focus on positive things
like his talents and pastimes.

Brian Dennis was seventeen.
He was kind
when he wanted to be.
Funny
without even trying.
He loved music,
especially hearing it live.
He liked to draw.
He was a great kisser.

I stop.
I'd like to be able to
write about his relationship
to his parents or his friends,
but I can't.
I'd like to be able to
write what was really important to Brian.
But I don't know that either.
Apparently, I don't know much.

Here we go again.

9:00 a.m.: Alarm goes off.

9:15 a.m.: Get out of bed.

9:18 a.m.: Shower.

9:25 a.m.: Pull wet hair into ponytail.

9:29 a.m.: Put on white shirt, black pants, and sneakers.

9:33 a.m.: Dab on concealer, brush on mascara.

9:40 a.m.: Eat bowl of cereal.

9:50 a.m.: Walk out front door.

10:00 a.m.: Arrive at Renzo's.

This is a new sort of routine.

Somewhere in between

the late lunch and early dinner crowd,

I ask Ethan about college.

He says,

"I might major in sociology or anthro.

Not sure which yet,

but definitely something

that involves studying people.

Have you thought about college?

It's about that time, right?"

"Yeah, it is.

I should be thinking

about it this summer,

but I've been distracted.

I might just apply to some state schools.

Or maybe take another year to decide."

"Aren't your parents on your ass about it?"

"Nah. My mom's not too bad.

But she does keep leaving college catalogs around.

I think she hopes they'll inspire me."

"And what about your dad?"

"He's not around . . .

So I never asked.

Where are you from?"

"Michigan."

"How come you didn't go home for the
summer?"

"And miss the chance

to work with you at Renzo's?
Just kidding."
As he says that,
he knocks his shoulder into mine.
"I'm taking a summer class
and renting a house with some guys.
Besides, home is not a good place
to be right now."

    "Oh," I say as I neaten a stack of napkins.
I'm curious about what he means,
but I don't want to ask —
especially since I changed the subject
when he asked about my dad.
But to my surprise,
he keeps going.
"My parents are getting divorced."

    "Oh.

    I'm so sorry."
"It's okay.
I'm just glad they're doing something
besides fighting.
I get it.
It took a while,
but I get it now.
They're not meant to be together.
Or maybe they were,
but only for twentysomething years.
Like their marriage had an expiration date."

I can't believe
Ethan's telling me this stuff.
Brian never talked about his family.
The most he ever said was:
"My dad'll be home soon,
you better go."

"Whoa. Look at you,"

Parker says when he walks into Renzo's.

"What do you mean?"

"In all the years I've known you,

I've never, ever

seen you in a polo shirt.

And it's white.

And tucked in!"

Parker is laughing so hard

that his face is turning red.

"Come on.

It's not that bad."

"You're right.

I suppose it could be worse.

It could be a poncho,"

he says, wiping tears from his eyes.

I shake my head and laugh with him.

It is a real laugh.

Not one I am trying on.

I am too tired
to visit Brian tonight.
After seven hours at Renzo's,
my arms and legs are sore
and I have a major headache.
I just want to go home
and wash my face
and get into bed.

I sleep
heavy,
hot,
and dreamless.

Sometimes I catch myself

starting to feel a little bit happy,
starting to look forward to things
like going back to school in a few weeks.
But then I am struck
with fear.
What if I get into a car accident
and get seriously hurt?
What if I die?
What if something terrible
happens to my mom
or one of my friends?
These thoughts creep
up on me.

The death book says
that when my thoughts race,
I should try to stay present.
To be where my feet are.
But I don't want
to be
where my feet are.
They still feel
for fault lines.

The death book wants me
to consider getting back to my routine —
to find myself again.
It wants to know if I am ready
to move on,
to try to get back to normal.
But I don't know
what normal is.

Jewish people
are meant to return to their routines
after seven days of mourning.
Muslims get three days
(longer, if a wife is mourning her husband),
and Hindus get thirteen days
after the deceased is cremated.
None of these
seem like enough time.

Ethan and I are last to leave work.
Even though I tell him I want to go home,
he insists that we go to the local carnival.
It comes every year at this time.
It's nothing fancy.
Skee-Ball, ring toss,
and a few mildly scary rides.

Before we walk over to the carnival,
Ethan changes out of his uniform
and into jeans and a rugby-type shirt.
This might be the first time
I've seen him in normal clothes.

At the carnival,
Ethan buys a roll of tickets
before I can even protest.
"Let's go on the Gravitron first,"
he says, pulling me
toward what looks like a spaceship.
Ethan hands the guy
enough tickets for the two of us,
and we go inside.
Cheesy techno music is blasting
as everyone finds a spot
and leans against the red-padded walls.
Once the ride is somewhat full,
the entrance doors dramatically clang shut.

The ride starts off spinning slowly.
But the longer and faster we spin,
the more we stick to the mats.
Everyone is laughing and screaming
because they can't
pick up their arms, legs, and head.
Based on the ride's name,
I suppose gravity's at work.
Maybe if I'd paid more attention
in science class
I'd know what was happening.

Ethan looks really happy.
He's laughing a deep belly laugh.
But all I can think is:
This feeling is familiar.
Feeling stuck.
Frozen.
I wonder
if I started crying,
would the tears freeze on my cheeks?
Or would they roll down,
defying gravity?
Thankfully, it's not long
before the ride slows
and I can pull myself
off the mat again.

When we step outside,
I'm a little dizzy.
Ethan sees that the ride hasn't affected me
the same way that it has him.
He's still smiling.
I must look green.
"Should we try something
where our feet stay on the ground?" he asks.

    "Sure," I say
    even though I'd rather go home
    or sit and talk to Brian.
But he's just too excited,
and I can't say no.   •
"Come on. I see Skee-Ball," he says.
I reluctantly follow behind him.
He's like a kid let loose in a toy store.
"You know, I'm pretty amazing at this."

    "Really? I suck.
    How about I just watch.
    Maybe I'll even cheer."
"Okay. Prepare to have your mind blown."

He sinks the ball into the forty pocket
over and over again.
Tickets are coming out of the side
of the machine like crazy.
I can't help but cheer.

"You're a Skee-Ball genius!
How'd you do that?"
"Raw talent, Annaleah,"
he says as he grabs all the tickets
and ushers me in the direction
of the prize counter.
"Your pick, cheerleader."
"Me? But you did all the work."
"It's okay. Giant Hello Kitties
aren't really my thing."
"All right, then. That one."
I point to a unicorn with a sparkly horn.
When the ticket guy gives me my prize,
I hug it tightly to my chest.

As Ethan walks me home,
I wonder,
Does he think this was a date?
It sort of feels like a date —
especially that last part
with the unicorn.
But he hasn't tried to kiss me
or hold my hand,
so maybe it isn't.
Just as I am wondering
if I even want it to be a date,
I see the edge of the cemetery.

I feel like I should duck behind a tree
so Brian doesn't see me.
It's like walking past the cemetery
with Ethan is cheating —
like I am doing something wrong.
Even though nothing has happened.

Ethan turns to me and says,
"I'm glad we finally hung out
somewhere that's not Renzo's."
But that's when he sees
that my eyes are full of tears.
"Oh, God, was tonight that bad?" he asks.
     "No, no, it's not that.
     It's just that,
     there was this guy.
     We were sort of together
     and then . . ."
"It's okay. I get it."
But there's no way he does.

We walk the last block to my house
in silence.
Ethan takes me to my door and says,
"See you at work tomorrow."
Then we hug awkwardly
with the unicorn smushed between us.

I go inside, but not upstairs.
I wait by the door for a minute,
then look out the window.
When Ethan's out of sight,
I slip back out the door.
I owe Brian an explanation.

"So that was Ethan.
He's the guy I told you about
from the pizza place.
This is the first time we've hung out
besides at work.
I shouldn't have to explain,
but I feel like I do.
Like you think
I was cheating on you.
I know that's crazy,
but that's how —"
The sound of footsteps
startles me into silence.
I turn and see a guy's silhouette
making its way toward me.
Even though the air is warm,
my body goes completely cold.

As the person strides closer,
the details of a face
come into view —
it's Peter.
Brian's closest friend.
I saw him speak at the funeral,
but we've never officially met.
"I thought I was the only one
who came at night,"
he says.

For the second time tonight
I feel as if I have been caught
doing something I shouldn't.
He sits down next to me and asks,
"How did you know Brian?"
I hope that what I am about to say
will be familiar to him.
That Brian talked about me.
That I meant more to him
than he let on.
     "We were
       kind of, sort of
       seeing each other."
"Oh. You're Sarah?"

His question wrecks me.
Wrecks all of the stories
I have told myself.
I didn't think it was possible
for words to hurt this much.
     "No.
       I'm Annaleah."
Peter sucks in air
through his teeth,
then lets it out really slowly.
"Oh, God.
I'm so sorry.
I didn't know you

and Brian were . . ."
But I'm already getting up.
  "I should let you
    be alone with Brian."

I don't know why
I'm surprised.
I shouldn't be.
I know Brian and I weren't
boyfriend and girlfriend.
I know that he was terrible
about calling me back
and making plans.
I knew he had a life
when he wasn't with me.
But all that dissolved
when we were together.

I wonder
who Sarah is.
I wonder
if she was at the funeral.
I wonder
if she's the blond Marissa saw.
I wonder
what Brian liked about her.
Is she prettier than me?
Funnier, smarter, sexier?
I get a flash
of Brian having sex with her,
and it is awful.
I can't be sure that they even had sex,

but it's definitely a possibility.
I feel like I am going to puke.

Was Peter telling me about Sarah

a sign from Brian?
If so, it was cruel.
He didn't need to do that.
He's already gone.
He didn't have to make it hurt more.
Or maybe it was the universe telling me?
Maybe it thought that this would help me
get over Brian.
Or was it just chance
that Peter and I were at the cemetery
at the same time?
Absolutely nothing otherworldly at work.
No greater purpose.
No sign.
Nothing.

I shut my eyes

and see a pocket of darkness.
I want to fold myself
flat and crisp,
slip inside of it
like a sheet of paper
into an envelope.

At work the next day I say,

"Ethan, I should explain
about last night."

"You don't have to."
"Yeah, I do.
You see,
I was sort of seeing this guy
and he died of this freak heart thing.
It only happened two months ago,
and I'm still trying
to figure everything out."

"I know."
"What do you mean
you *know?*"

"I know about Brian."
I am so confused by hearing Ethan
say Brian's name
that anger
doesn't set in right away.
"I don't understand.
How do you know
about Brian?"

"I heard your girlfriends talking about it
while you were in the back.
And then I remembered
reading about his death in the paper."
He must be talking about
when Marissa and Jessica were here.

"You've known basically since I started
and didn't tell me?"

   "I figured you'd bring it up
   when you were ready.
   I don't understand, Annaleah.
   I thought it was the right thing to do."

"You know, I knew
there was a reason
you were being so nice to me,"
I say, backing away from him.

   "What?
   It's nothing like that.
   I like you.
   You're interesting."

"Interesting . . . right.
Like a sociology experiment?
Did you want to study
a real, live, grieving girl?"

   "Annaleah —"

"I better check on my tables."

   "Annaleah, wait."

But I don't.

In bed, I cannot sleep.
I think about my dad
calling on my last birthday.

When I pick up the phone,
he doesn't say hello.
He just starts singing in a goofy voice.
When he's done he asks,
"So, do you know
what your birthday wish
is going to be?"
He asks me the same thing every year.
    "No. I haven't decided yet."
I roll over and look at my alarm clock.
    "Dad, it's really really early."
"I know.
I just wanted to be the first person
you talked to today."
    "You're definitely the first."
"Okay, baby.
Go back to bed."
    "Thanks, Dad.
    Love you."
"Love you too."

When I hang up the phone,
I pull the covers over my head,

block out the early morning light,
wrap my arms around my pillow,
and sleep
sleep
sleep.

It's hard not to speak to someone

when speaking to them is part of your job.
For the next few days,
I only speak to Ethan about pizza.
I refuse to acknowledge him
in any other way.
Instead of chatting with him
when it's slow,
I make napkin wraps.
I fill salt and pepper shakers.
I wipe down already clean tables.
I sit in a booth
and count the tiles on the wall.
Any of these things is better
than talking to Ethan.

Before, I didn't have anything to say.

Nothing was happening.

There was only death.

There was only Brian.

I finally have something to say.

I call Parker.

I tell him about Sarah.

I tell him about Ethan

knowing about Brian.

"All that in twenty-four hours, Lee?

Sounds intense."

 "Yeah."

"I have two theories.

Wanna hear them?"

 "I don't know.

 Do I?"

"I'm gonna tell you anyway.

One: It's heinous

that Brian was seeing someone else.

But you've got to keep it in perspective —

you weren't officially together."

 "Thanks for the news flash.

 What's two?"

"I think you overreacted

when Ethan told you he knew about Brian."

 "But he lied," I snap.

"He didn't lie, Lee.

He respected your feelings.
Apparently, there are still guys
who do that."

    "But I feel
    like he had ulterior motives."
"To do what? Become your friend?
Take you to a carnival? Have fun?
How shocking!
Someone should arrest him
before he befriends someone else!"

    "Not funny, Parker.
    I don't want to be someone's friend
    just because they feel bad for me."
"Whoever said that was his reason?
Did it ever occur to you
that he might like you
just because
you're you?"

I don't have an answer.

"So what's your plan, Lee?
Are you going to keep ignoring
the nice, thoughtful, cute boy?"

I decide to call.
I know it's time.
I know I have to do this.

As I hit SEND on my phone,
I feel humbled.
Like I am slinking back
after having done something
terribly wrong.

Now the phone is ringing
and I'm wondering if it's too late,
if maybe Marissa
won't want to be friends anymore.

Marissa and I agree

to go to the movies.
The movie was my idea.
I suggested it because it seemed safe.
We could be together,
but not have to talk the whole time.

I'm not sure
how all this is going to go down.
Probably not like Brian's funeral.
That was our one day of grace —
like she hadn't freaked out
when I told her that Brian and I had sex,
like she hadn't said really hurtful things,
like we hadn't gone weeks without talking.

And now we're back to weirdness again.
And this time,
it's my fault.

The movie is perfect.
It's a comedy about a bunch of guys
driving cross-country
and all the hilariously stupid
things that happen along the way.
It requires no thought.
It is a ninety-minute
vacation from my brain.

When the movie is over,
Marissa drives us to the diner.
Just like we used to,
we order coffee and cheese fries.
It's nice
that some things don't change.
But the conversation isn't easy.
We start by talking about the movie.
But that doesn't last long.

She asks, "So, how's work?"
    "It's okay.
    Just something to do,
    you know.
    What have you been up to?"
"Working almost every day for the Grants.
Steven is walking.
And Dana's talking up a storm."
    "Whoa. That happened fast."

"Well, not really."
That feels like an intentional jab.
But she's right.
Had Marissa and I been talking,
I would have known these things.

She asks, "How are you feeling?"
    "Okay. Better. Sort of.
    It's hard.
    And the last week
    has been tough."
"Why? What happened?"

I want to tell her
about finding out about Sarah.
I want to be close to her again,
but I don't want her to say
I told you so.
I don't want her to even think it.
So I only tell her about Ethan.

"And now you're not talking to him?"
    "Yeah."
"Really?"
She pauses.
"I know things haven't been good
between us.
But I have to say this:

You're doing it again."
    "Doing what?"
"Shutting people out.
People who want to be there for you."

I try to take this in.

"Annaleah, you've got to talk to me
because I can't even imagine
what it's been like since Brian died.
Or what it's like
to have a dad that walked out
and hasn't even called in fifteen years.
You never talk about any of these things.
That can't be good for you."

Her words challenge me.
They challenge all the stories
I've told myself.

"But there are people that you do have.
You have me.
You have Parker.
You have Joy.
And maybe you have Ethan.
Don't ignore us."

I want to get up and leave.
I want to go and sit in the cemetery.

I want to tell Brian about this.
I want him to listen
and to not speak.
I want to climb into bed
and think about my dad.
Think about all the things
that could have been.
But I stay.
I stay
and listen to Marissa.

As a kid, there were a few times

when I asked my mom about my dad.
She always answered as best she could.

"We met and married quickly.
It wasn't long before
our foundation
started showing cracks.
When you were about one,
he left — not honoring
any promises he'd made."
    "But don't you want to find him?
    To know what he is doing?"
"Yes, of course.
But I don't want to look for someone
who doesn't want to be found.
I don't want someone
who doesn't want me.
If he wanted to find us
he would have, could have.
But he clearly doesn't want to.
It's been over a decade."
    "But —"
"No 'but.'
I've got to go on.
I've got to deal with what's here,
what's in front of me.

And that's you, Annaleah.
That's my friends, my job."

Her words were never enough for me.
Not knowing
was not acceptable.
That father-shaped space
needed to be filled,
even if it was filled with fiction.

As we are paying the check,

Marissa says, "I'm sorry
for being so hard on you about Brian
when you were together.
I didn't want you to get hurt
and everything I said
kept coming out wrong.
I want to be close again.
I've missed you."

 "I've missed you too."
"Life's boring without you.
You know, I haven't
missed a single curfew this summer!"

 "Yeah, well,
 I haven't even been to any parties."
"We should change that.
Have some fun.
Take a mini road trip or something.
Do you think we can
just go forward from here?
I'll try to be less bitchy,
promise."

 "And I'll try to be
 less . . .
 absent, I promise."

Instead of going home,
I ask Marissa to drop me off at the cemetery.
As I walk toward Brian's grave
I think about how I believed
that my stories made the Dearly Departed
feel less lonely
and more loved.
But these people don't need me.
Each stone represents a lifetime of stories —
stories that existed before me,
stories that will exist after I'm gone.
I was the one who needed the stories.
I was the one who needed to feel
less lonely and more loved.

"Back so soon?" Brian's grandmother asks

as she comes up beside me.

"Yeah. I guess so,"

I say even though I've been here

so many times since she saw me last.

"Looks like you've got the right idea sitting.

Down isn't so much the problem.

Will you give me a lift in a little while?"

"Sure," I say

as she awkwardly lowers herself down.

"Hello there, Brian.

I'm with your nice friend, Annaleah.

You're missing a beautiful day here.

But I bet it's real nice where you are too.

You be sure to say hello to my Joey.

And let him know

that I am thinking about him too."

I've never heard anyone speak

at a graveside like this before.

Like me.

Freda sees my amazement.

"Do you talk to him too?" she asks.

"Sometimes."

"I think talking

about good times helps.

What do you say?"

There were
good times.
But there were bad times too.
And a lot of nothing times.
   "All sorts of things, I guess.
   But mostly, what it's like
   without him."
"You were more than just friends."
She doesn't ask it.
She says it.
The recognition
that I've been waiting for.
Tears well up in my eyes.
"Do you come to talk to him a lot?"
   "Almost every day."
"Oh, honey," she says
as she takes my hand in hers.
"It's important to remember Brian,
to keep him in your heart,
and to visit with him.
But this isn't a place for every day.
Nothing grows here
besides grass."
She moves her hand to my back
and alternately rubs and pats.
I am crying harder now.
I don't want her to feel me shaking,

but I don't want her to take her hand away either.
I look around and think about what she said:
Nothing grows here.
She's right.
This isn't a place for growth.
It's a place to look back on the past.

I cannot control
that my dad left.
I cannot control
that Brian died.
But I can control
if I choose to maintain my friendships.
I can control
if I try to be closer to my mom.
I can control
whether or not
I get to know Ethan better.

There are spaces in my heart
that are being filled
by what could have been with Brian,
and the stories
about my father and the Dearly Departed.
I think I need to free up some of that space
for the people in my life
that are actually here.
I need to not keep that space reserved
for people who are never coming.

I slide a napkin across the counter.

Across it I've written,

I'm sorry for being such a freak.

Ethan picks it up and smiles.

"Are you okay?" he asks.

"I don't know.

Yes. No. Maybe."

"Are we okay?"

"Yes."

"All right, then . . .

here are your slices for table seven."

And just like that,

we are

okay.

The death book wants me
to write a happy list —
the small things in life
that make me happy.
The first thing on the book's sample list
is puppies and kittens.
I can't help but laugh.
Are they kidding?
But I guess laughing
puts me in a better mood to do this.
So here goes:

Garlic knots.
Soft sheets that smell like detergent.
Stars in a clear night sky.
Getting texts from friends.
Fireflies and crickets.
Brian's eyes.
Strawberry ice cream.
Sitting in the sun.
My jeans with the hole in the knee.
Making friends laugh.
Seeing Ethan smile.
Sun showers.
My beat-up white Converse.
Pink roses in bloom.

"Do you want it to be more?"

Joy asks as we sit on her bed.

    "I don't know.

    Ethan is fun to be around.

    And cute. But —"

"Lee, it's not like you need to decide

if you want to marry him.

It's more simple.

Are you curious to see

where it might go?"

Where can it go?

All sorts of tragic scenes come to mind.

Car accidents. Fires.

Ethan disappearing.

Me being left, devastated.

    "I don't know if I'm ready.

    I don't think I could handle

    the disappointment."

"Lee, you can handle a lot.

You made it through this summer.

What could be harder than that?"

    "I guess."

"So what are you going to do?"

    "I don't know.

    I'll think about it."

Joy throws a glittery pillow at my head.

"Thinking never got anyone anywhere."

Sitting next to Ethan,
eating lunch in the back.
We are squeezed together.
His shirt is touching my arm.
Our knees are inches from each other.
I want to close the gap,
the painful gap.
I cross my legs the other way
to fill the space.
My knee lands against his.
Contact.
I can finally breathe.

There is this one page in the death book
that talks about relaxation.
It suggests that when you are in bed
you try imagining
being on a beach or in a field
with the warm sun on your face.
I never did the exercise,
but right now I'm on a work break,
actually sitting outside in the sun,
so I give it a try.

I shut my eyes
and try to remember what the book said —
something about letting in the rays of sunlight
to help get rid of the dark.
Immediately, the *Sesame Street* theme song
creeps into my head and makes me smile:
"*Sunny day, sweepin' the clouds away . . .*"
Okay. Focus.
This is serious.

I shut my eyes again.
I feel the sun hitting my face,
warming the top of my head.
Behind my eyelids, all I see is bright yellow.
The longer I sit,
the brighter the yellow grows,
the warmer I feel.

The more the tension in my shoulders
melts away.
I try to focus only on that —
the warmth and the yellow.
And for a few moments,
that's all there is.

Ethan and I both have the afternoon off.

He asks me if I want
to hang out
and I say yes.

Being with Ethan
feels different.
Talking to him
and having him
talk back to me.
Looking at him
and having him
look back at me.
And then there are the times
when we touch.
They're just accidental bumps
or nudges,
but it feels amazing.

We stop and sit.
The grass is speckled with dandelions,
the kind that have turned white and poofy.
I pick one up,
twirl the stem between my fingers.
"Make a wish," he says.
    "Really?"
"Go on. I'll do it too."
We both pause for a moment,

then blow.
The seeds scatter in the air,
then float back down like tiny parachutes.
"What'd you wish for?" he asks.

    "I can't tell you.

    It won't come true."
"Well, fine then.
I won't tell you my wish either."
He fake-pouts like a little kid.

It's getting late,
nearly dinner when Ethan says,
"I better go.
I'm having people over tonight —
kind of an end-of-summer party.
You should come,
if you can."

My body buzzes

as I try to get dressed for Ethan's party.
I can't decide what to wear,
mostly because I am too busy
imagining what it'd be like to kiss him.
This image makes my heart
flutter.
It makes between my legs
flutter.

I feel all of this energy
going through me.
I have not been able to sit still all night.
My fingers tap the table.
My toes tap the floor.
I cannot focus.
My chest feels tight
but instead of anxiety,
I feel excitement.

At the party, I find Ethan

standing on his back deck,
wearing an untucked button-down and jeans.
It's a treat to see him again in real clothes
and not those horrid checkered pants.
Crowds of people are around
and below him.
But he seems sort of oblivious.
He's just staring up at the dark sky.
He sees me coming and nods at the stars,
"Should we make a wish?"

    "What's with you and the wishes today?"
He just shrugs and points up into the darkness.
"I'm wishing on that one.
Which one are you going to wish on?"

    "That one,"
    I say, pointing upward.
We are quiet for a moment
before he asks,
"So . . . what'd you wish for?"

    "Ethan, we've been through this."
"Okay, okay," he says.
"How about we each
write down our wish,
then exchange.
When we are both home
and getting into bed,
we can look."

I laugh.
I didn't figure him for the cheesy type.
　　"All right," I say
and he goes into the house
and comes back with paper and pens.
I write:
I wish that we had kissed this afternoon.
My heart races as I write those eight words.
I think about ripping up the paper
and rewriting something less risky,
but don't.
I take a deep breath,
take his note,
and he takes mine.

After hanging out for a little while,
I head home.
Partly because I don't know anyone there
besides Ethan and Lou.
But mostly because I'm dying to read the note.

I can feel it in my back pocket.
It is an itch on my skin
that I have to scratch.
The farther I walk from Ethan's house,
the more the itch begins to burn.
I make it three blocks before I stop
and take the note out of my pocket.
As I unfold it, my heart pounds.
I'm excited to see what it says.
I hope that it's about me,
but I'm scared
that it will be something dumb, like
I *wish for world peace*,
and I will be humiliated.

And then the note is open
and I am reading it
and it says: To kiss you.
And before I realize it,
I am running.
Running

the three blocks back to Ethan's house,
and then I am through his front door,
scanning the faces, looking for him.
And then I am out the back door,
and on the back deck.
I see Lou and ask if he's seen Ethan.
He says he saw him in the backyard.
And then I am down the stairs,
and searching for Ethan's face again.
He doesn't see me coming at first,
but when he does, he looks confused.
In one quick motion,
I put my hand on his chest,
push him into the shadows under the deck,
and then I am kissing him.
And it is amazing.
Just the right mix
of hard and soft.
After a little while,
I can feel him smiling,
and I pull back.
"You cheated," he says.
"You didn't wait until you got home."
    "You didn't look?"
"No. Should I look now?"
    "Yes."
He reads the note, smiles,

then puts one hand on the side of my face,
the other on my neck,
and kisses me.
It is warm
and it is real.

The death book wants me

to write a letter to Brian in heaven.

Dear Brian,
The last few months
have been a roller coaster.
Meeting you
and starting to get to know you
was really exciting.
But there were limits
on how close you let me get.
And I guess I did a bit of the same.

When we were together,
I was willing to take whatever you gave.
And after you died
I was able to see
how little that was.

I deserved
and still deserve
more.
I'm not sorry or regretful
about us.
There were good times.
I learned things about myself.
And it also made me see that memories —

real or imagined —
can't make me whole.

I'll never know
why you were the way you were.
I'll never know if it was because of your dad.
Or if it was because you didn't
like me enough.
But I'm going to have to learn
to be okay with not knowing.

Brian, I want you to be at peace
and I want that for myself too.
And I don't think I'll get that
if I keep visiting you like I have been.
It keeps me from growing.
So I'm writing to you
to tell you that I'm not
going to come around for a while.
I'll still think of you.
You'll still be the first guy
I ever really cared about.
But I've got to let you go.

Now what?
It's not like I can look up
the address for heaven in the White Pages

and put a stamp on this
and drop it in the mail.

I know this letter was for me.
But I still want to do something with it.
The death book suggests
that I fold it into a paper airplane
or put it in a bottle and send it out to sea.
But I have another idea.

It feels a little ridiculous

to be standing at Brian's grave
when I just wrote that I wouldn't
be coming here anymore.
It feels very ridiculous
to be standing at Brian's grave
and holding a soup spoon.
But leaving the letter here,
in the ground above Brian,
seems like the right place.

The dirt is still a bit uneven,
but now there are lots of wisps of grass
sprouting up from it.
I crouch down and lean forward
as if I am about to whisper Brian a secret,
and begin to dig.
After about ten scoops,
I roll the letter up
and drop it into the hole.
I fill the hole back in,
stand up, step back,
and walk away.

I had to be ready.
I wasn't.
I had to want my life back.
I didn't.
But I do now.
I can't flip a switch
and make things go back to normal.
But I can try.

I need to remind myself
to make phone calls,
to seek out my friends.
So after staring at my contacts list,
I finally hit SEND.
"Hey, Maris. What's up?" I ask.
    "Hi! I'm racing to get to yoga."
"Oh, okay. Well, we can —"
    "Do you want to come?"
My instinct is to say no.
Or to lie and say I have plans
so I can spend the afternoon in bed.
But I fight it.
"Yeah. Okay. I'll go."
    "Cool. Pick you up in five."

It's been a while since I've done yoga.
At first everything hurts,
is stiff,
and all the talk
about heart centers,
energy, and breath
seems so strange —
not at all where my thoughts have been.

During tree pose,
I try to clear my mind
and balance on one foot,

but I wobble, I tip.
The instructor says,
"Breathe easy. Maintain focus."
But I can't seem to do either —
especially since Marissa is watching me
out of the corner of her eye, grinning.
I don't know how, but she manages
to maintain the pose perfectly,
even while she laughs at me.
This makes me laugh
and wobble even more.

When we go into pigeon pose
I feel a sharp pain in my thigh.
So, just like the instructor said,
I stop and go into child's pose.
I fold over, my chest on my thighs,
my arms at my sides,
and feel the weight
of my body
sinking into the floor.
And just breathe
breathe
breathe.